A MINOR OPERATION

Books by Gene Rontal

A Pre-Existing Condition

The Police Surgeon

Sterile Justice

A Lethal Dose

The Cruelest Cut

A MINOR OPERATION

A Detective Ben Dailey, M.D. Mystery

GENE RONTAL

Bellingham, WA

bookhouse
PUBLISHING

2950 Newmarket St., Suite 101-358 | Bellingham, WA 98226
Ph: 206.226.3588 | www.bookhouserules.com

A Minor Operation
Copyright © 2025 by Gene Rontal

This is a work of fiction. Names, characters, places, brands, media, and incidents are either the product of the author's imagination or are used fictitiously.

10 9 8 7 6 5 4 3 2 1

Library of Congress Control Number: 2025909576

ISBN: 978-1-952483-76-9 (Paperback)
ISBN: 978-1-952483-77-6 (eBook)

Editor: Julie Scandora
Book design: Scott Book & Melissa Vail Coffman

*It is not the strongest of the species that survives,
nor the most intelligent that survives.
It is the one that is the most adaptable to change.*

PROLOGUE

Looking at the fierce blizzard covering the parking lot, two friends in parkas stood inside the entrance of a restaurant. To some it could have been a cartoon artist's delight, like Mutt and Jeff. One was a tall handsome man, Anthony Reynolds, the well-known congressman from Southeast Michigan. He was rubbing a thick beard. The other man was Michael Edwards, a heavy-set man with a paper cup in his hands as he was taking down the remnant of his Miller High Life. Edwards knew everything about his friend and was Reynold's assistant in his plan to climb to the US Senate. While they talked, all they saw were cars like tents in the deep drifts of wet snow. The combination of snow and rain seems to last every year forever in the Midwest. The local weathermen call it "snain."

People in the restaurant noticed the Senate candidate. He was like a hero to the community, and they swarmed Reynolds with questions. But when they finished their discussions with him after having had their dinners and a couple of the local brews, all—including Edwards and Reynolds—agreed it was time to get their money's worth from their fancy Range Rovers and get the hell out of this parking lot. As soon as they walked out the door, rain and snow pelted them in horizontal waves. Just managing to stand upright, they ran to their vehicles and began scraping off the hard snow, giving them a chance to stay warm and to reconsider leaving for home.

Anxious and disconcerted, Reynolds climbed into his Rover and shouted to himself, "What the hell am I doing out here in the middle of this storm?"

Edwards and many of the others joined Reynolds back inside the restaurant to discuss the weather. The storm showed no evidence of stopping. Large drifts of snow now blocked their view from the windows. But all finally decided to leave, although they knew it was going to be hard to get home.

Reynold told Edwards, "This is the worst day of the year to be on the Rouge River Drive."

While they continued talking, Edwards got coffee in a paper cup from a machine for each of them, along with sugar and a couple of energy bars. He told Reynolds to follow him home. Then both hustled for their SUVs, restarted their engines, and again cleaned off their windshields. Reynolds removed a frozen piece of paper that was stuck by ice on his windshield. Irritated, he found out it was a newspaper and quickly scraped off the rest. Before climbing into their vehicles, Edwards said they were going to drive down the road.

As they left, they passed a couple of stranded cars in the parking lot. Reynolds made sure to drive his SUV close behind Edwards's Rover. Ten minutes later, in spite of his braking and adjusting of the steering wheel, Edwards could barely control the forward motion of his powerful SUV. Meanwhile, Reynolds closed his gap with Edwards's SUV. When Reynolds was within fifty feet, he decided he was close enough and accelerated his Rover, bumping into Edwards's car and causing it to swerve on the icy road. That was followed by a high-pitched shout from Edwards and a curse from him for the absence of the city's salt trucks. Then Edwards lost control and slid to the top of the embankment above the Rouge River. His braking lights lit up, but his car suddenly slid down toward the river. He tried to stop, but braking was useless as his vehicle continued its inexorable trip into the icy river. In a panic, he took off his hat and glanced at a bright light in the rearview mirror. "Help," he thought. Then he totally lost control, and his SUV headed straight for the Rouge River.

At the bottom of the embankment, there was a huge, gnarly maple tree next to the river with large leafless branches pointing at the windshield of Edwards's falling vehicle. Edwards couldn't avoid hitting the branches. Suddenly the windshield cracked, and many pieces of glass flew into his face. Several of them struck in his neck.

Edwards soon felt a warm liquid finding its way down his chest. Drifting in and out of consciousness, he tried to gain control and stop the bleeding with his coat, but it didn't work. He was losing blood too fast and fainted.

Reynolds had stayed on the road and appeared to be in charge of the drive in the storm as he moved down the road for another half-mile. His SUV now became the only vehicle on the road. Ahead there was a sign for a park maintenance station and a driveway. He pulled into the driveway, waited ten minutes, and then turned around, heading back to the spot where Edwards had gone over the embankment. He stopped, put on rubber boots, and holding on to a few trees, managed to get out of his vehicle and walk down the embankment near Edwards's damaged SUV. Once there, Reynolds took out a flashlight and shined the light through the side window. Edwards's head was slumped over the steering wheel. Using his flashlight, he put on rubber gloves, opened the door, and checked the driver inside. He felt for a pulse. There was none.

Satisfied, Reynolds nodded.

Then he found a broken branch on the embankment and used it to climb back to his vehicle. As he walked a few steps up, he slipped in the muddy snow and fell on a sharp rock. He noted pain in his right hand. Once he took off his glove, he saw he had cut his hand on a piece of glass from the windshield, and it began to bleed. Reynolds reached into his jacket and pulled out a white handkerchief to stop the bleeding. When he controlled it, he took another step. Unfortunately, he didn't realize the deepness of the mud and snow and slipped, accidently dropping his handkerchief. The blizzard so obscured vision, that even with his flashlight, he couldn't find it. Reynolds stood there, cursing the storm, not wanting to leave a bloody handkerchief and have it found by some unknown person. After twenty more minutes of searching, all the while getting wetter and colder, he gave up and climbed the embankment back to the road. The rain and snow, still falling, were washing his footsteps away. When he reached the road, he could barely see the road. There were still no other vehicles, except his Rover.

Figuring the handkerchief would get buried deep in snow and mud, he didn't worry about it. Once Reynolds was inside his SUV, he turned on the engine, and with the shelter from snow, the heat from the motor made him he feel safe—and confident. Edwards was no longer alive, and no one saw him do anything that would connect him to Edwards's death. He smiled for a moment knowing the people in his district idolized him. He was clean for his chance to be in the Senate in Washington, DC.

Reynolds took fifteen minutes to drive to the expressway. At the intersection, he saw a snowplow, blade down, shoving snow and dirt off the road that led to the river.

Chapter 1

"This is just a minor operation, isn't it, Doc?"

"George, just so you know, a minor operation is an operation done on somebody else. Remember, George, when it comes to you, it's a major procedure. In medicine, any procedure can go wrong." I smiled. "But just to put you at ease, I've never lost anyone doing this operation."

Homicide Lieutenant George Sennett worked in the Detroit Police Department. He was my best friend. Sennett's presence in the operating chair was because of a broken nose he obtained as the result of a routine exercise session in the station. He had shrugged his shoulders and said it was just part of the job.

Now as I spoke, I took a pair of surgical gloves off an instrument stand, picked a cotton pledget with forceps, dipped it into the blue solution on the table, and placed it in Sennett's nose. "George, did I ever tell you that I broke my nose in college playing football?"

"No. Is this going to be one of your war stories?"

"Kinda. The most I got on the team was third string, mostly on the practice squad. However, I did get into a game because the guy ahead of me had a leg cramp. No big deal, all I had to do was to take on the other team's All-American left tackle. We were running a jet sweep. I blocked him and he stunted. I tried to recover, but he bent his elbow on my face guard. The straps weren't supposed to release, but they did, and his face mask came down on my nose. Ergo, the Dailey nose."

Sennett laughed. "And all this time I thought you'd had a nose job. By the way, what's that blue stuff you put in my nose?"

"Cocaine."

"What! I'm clean They won't let me back into the hospital!"

"Relax. Cocaine is a great anesthetic and decongestant of the nose."

"You're a doctor, right?"

"I think so. Would you like to see my diploma? At least that's what my diploma says. My theory is do the right thing, and you get the right solution. It doesn't hurt, right? I'm not from the no-pain-no-gain school. George, as I said, you are my best friend, and we have solved many tough situations. After a few minutes, this will calm things down. The pharmacist said he would give me all the precautions you need. Okay?"

Sennett nodded.

I handed the pharmacist's phone to Sennett.

After a couple of minutes, he handed the phone back to me and said, "You know that in today's situations you have to be careful with the cocaine."

"Relax," I said.

"I will," Sennett replied "After everything we've done over the over the years, Ben, I feel there was always trust between us."

"You're right. If I didn't trust you, I wouldn't be standing here. I just wanted to get my two words in for the record."

Sennett listened and then put the phone down. "Don't worry, Ben. The pharmacist said the same thing you told me."

"By the way," I said, "how did you break your nose?"

"I'd like to say it was something exciting, Ben, but it was my fault. We had a training session. I was trying to help teach this rookie. He was using a baton, and he didn't see me as I turned my head. The rest is history."

By now, I had injected a syringe of xylocaine and epinephrine, and at this point the inside of Sennett's nose was anesthetized with cocaine. Ten minutes later, I asked my nurse, Linda, to give me a slim metal instrument called a Cottle elevator. I slipped the probe through Sennett's nostril, found the crack in his nasal septum (the cartilage that separates the two sides of the nose), and gently pushed on the septum until it snapped back into a proper position. With the septum in place, I manipulated the nasal bones into the correct position and, with gloved hands, placed a light plaster cast on the nose to keep it in place. When I finished, Sennett's nose looked straight, and he was breathing well. I left the light plaster cast on the outside of the nose as an effort to remind Sennett to leave his nose alone. "It's all over, George. But please, try not to let anyone sneak up on you and punch you on your nose."

"Yeah, right. I look like I'm from one of those zombie movies. Nobody will get within two feet of me."

I was going to tell him to take two aspirins and call me in the morning, but my office manager, Karen, came back in the room.

"Dr. Dailey, you have a phone call," she said.

"Get the number and I'll call back."

Karen was silent for a moment. "I think you'd better take this one. It's Jordan."

A shiver ran down my back. She's my wife, and she was pregnant. When I'd left home that morning, she'd said she had some abdominal cramping. So now I quickly went back to my office and picked up the phone.

"Ben," Jordan said, "I'm going to City Hospital. My water broke. I can't get to St. Vincent's. I called Tom Bromley. He said he was there. Dorothy is going to take me."

"What about Joey?"

"I called the school. Dorothy is going to pick him up there."

I'd been through something like this before. Joey, our miracle child, had survived a near-death experience while Jordan was pregnant. No one said he'd survive. Now he was a healthy grade schooler. "I'm on my way," I said.

As I returned to Sennett, I was trying to decide whether he could get Jordan to the hospital in time in such awful traffic and horrendous weather. The snowfall had turned into a dense blizzard—not the best of driving conditions. This pregnancy was special because Jordan and I had been told we would never have another child. The child she was now carrying was from a frozen embryo, legally given to us by a woman who arranged through an attorney to make us guardians if anything happened to her. The tragedy was the mother was murdered. The murderer was captured, and now the child was going to be delivered. I looked at Sennett and told him what was going on.

Massaging the side of his head as if he was weary, Sennett then took charge. "Relax, Ben. We'll take my car from the office pool. It's made for this kind of weather. Besides, you have just operated on me. You need to take it easy, and I'll be quiet."

Chapter 2

Sennett got behind the wheel and put on the flasher. Debating logic with Lieutenant George Sennett, Detroit Homicide was usually fruitless unless you had a pretty good argument. And I did. Because of the cocaine, I couldn't let him drive. So I got behind the wheel, grabbed tightly onto the steering wheel, and sped off. But to me, we seemed to be standing still. " Why won't this heap go any faster?"

Sennett shook his head. "Well, you're in a cop car. Put on the siren and flash the lights."

I popped a Juicy Fruit in my mouth and started chewing hard enough to hear my molars grind. "Hell," I thought, "this is my wife, and it's going to be our baby." But this wasn't the first time I'd been in a car on a mission with Sennett. I had a badge from the Detroit Police Department with "Ben Dailey, Police Surgeon" on it. "This car must be that one from the loaner pool," I said. "Besides, they don't like it when we do all this kind of stuff when it's not company business."

Sennett clenched the muscles in his jaw. It was joined by his well-known scowl stamped on the brow above his eyes.

"George, maybe we can make an exception in driving. It's not every day that I'm going to be a father."

After a couple of minutes, Sennett nodded. "Okay, Ben. Are you ready for the two-corner option?"

"What the hell is that?" I asked as a green light appeared in the distance.

"Just make sure your seatbelt is working, follow my directions, and you'll see," he growled.

I nodded silently.

As the stop light came closer and we entered no man's land, Sennett silently picked up the baton from the front seat. His bulging forearms and the meat hooks he called his hands gripped the wooden instrument so hard that the blood in his fingers disappeared. "Push on it," he said.

The speedometer quickly registered sixty. We made it through the intersection just as the light turned yellow.

"It's okay, Ben, " Sennett said. "I didn't say I wanted to see the kid in heaven."

"Don't worry," I said. "Jordan will know wherever I am."

"What do you mean?"

"She gave me one of those tracking devices that you attach to your cell phone. No worries. She wanted to know where I am twice a day. I told her to check regularly to see where I am and call me any time."

Sennett shook his head as if he was clearing it from his "minor operation" and looked out the front windshield. A hint of a grin creased his face.

"I'm driving, but right now you're the boss," I said.

"That's where the two-corner option comes from. I learned it from Jimmy Rose at the academy. He was the instructor who taught me how to tail a suspect. The first thing he said is to know the habits of your target—where and when he works, what grocery store he shops at, any schools he attends, that kind of thing. Turn at the next light."

I quickly turned left, squealing the tires as we went through the intersection.

"Jimmy always said, 'If you know the landscape, you'll have a better idea of what your options are.' You don't want to tip anyone who might be following you. So stay at a distance."

"I don't get it," I said.

"When you want to get somewhere fast, every street corner with a stoplight has three options—stop, drive straight, or turn. All you have to remember is to keep your eye on your destination and keep the car moving in that direction to avoid the red light."

I followed his instructions, remaining silent as I drove and concentrated on the streetlights. Although it still didn't make sense to me, I didn't want to get into a logic discussion.

"Just make the turns," Sennett said, "and I'll conduct the drive."

Within ten minutes, we were at the front door of St. Vincent's Hospital. To me, the hospital was an anachronism. It was the site of both the near ruination of my career and the place of my greatest professional triumphs. I parked the car in front of the emergency room entrance, and Sennett flashed his badge at the hospital guard at the door. The lieutenant was an imposing man with smooth dark skin, serious eyes under heavy eyebrows, and a muscular neck, the result of playing linebacker in college. The cast that covered his nose made him look even more imposing. I followed.

Over time, I had learned Sennett wasn't all that imposing. When he told stories with a deep engaging voice and flashed his white teeth, it was hard not to like him. Besides, the two of us had a history together, one that kept us bonded for life.

The triage nurse looked nervous as the two men charged toward her, especially seeing Sennett with a splint on his nose. That changed quickly when I asked where Jordan Dalkind was.

"And who would you be, sir?" she replied as her eyes squinted and her brow lowered.

"I'm her husband, Ben Dailey," I replied as I rubbed the back of my neck. I knew the nurse was confused with the different last names, but Jordan had wanted to keep her name because of her profession as a federal attorney for the Southeast Michigan District.

"Dr. Dailey, your wife is in the emergency delivery room. If you want to see what's going on, you'd better hurry. It's lucky the storm has let up a little." Now friendly, the nurse smiled and pointed the way to the delivery room. "Good luck."

I turned the corner and made my way to the delivery room. I found Jordan on a gurney, lying with her head on a pillow and her knees bent. An IV was in her arm, and her obstetrician, Tom Bromley, stood in scrubs at her side. When Jordan saw her husband, her eyes lit up, and a smile spread over her face.

"I don't think I've ever seen a more beautiful woman in the world," I told myself.

"I thought you wouldn't make it," she said. Then she looked up at Sennett with his cast and the suggestion of a black eye.

"The doc was fixing me up when the nurse called that you were in the hospital," he explained.

In an emotionally rich voice, she said, "Well, I'm glad you got him here."

"I was just testing if you believed in that old navy saying," Sennett said.

"What do you mean by that?" Jordan asked.

"You gotta be there for the layin' of the keel, but you don't have to be there for the launching."

"Very funny. Do you really want to start quoting the navy handbook of etiquette?" she asked.

"Sorry if I sound like a jerk. I just wanted you to know I'm one with the people and trying to stay calm."

"Well, if you feel that way, you could always change places with me, and then you won't have to worry."

Bromley and Sennett both chuckled softly on that one. They knew the truth, that the baby was an embryo implant from a donor named Sandra Wells.

The humor didn't last too long.

I squeezed my fingernails into my hand and walked back with Tom into the room. Jordan still had her knees up and her head resting on a pillow, but I noticed she was biting her lips and shifting in the bed as if she couldn't get comfortable. This time she was the first to speak.

"Tom said that he may be able to turn the baby. I'd like to try that first rather than a C-section."

"You mean the same way he delivered Joey?"

I turned to Tom and asked if were there any problems.

He looked directly into my eyes with his hands held loosely behind his back. "The risks are not great, Ben. I think we could try an ECV. It's your and Jordan's decision."

I gave him a blank look. "You forgot I'm just a head and neck doctor. Talk English and explain it to Jordan and me."

Leaning over Jordan's gurney, he said, "Sorry, it's an external cephalic procedure where we manipulate the baby from outside and turn the baby's head down. If it doesn't work, we might have to do a C-section. It's exactly what we did with Joey."

I knew this wasn't my decision alone. That's why Jordan felt secure with Bromley as her doctor. I had made difficult decisions on patients many times as a physician. I know nothing is for sure in medicine, and the patient needs guidance.

Jordan listened, looked me directly in the eye, and asked me what she should do. I told her Tom Bromley is the best obstetrician in town and that's who we depend on.

Tom turned to look up at me. "Ben, you and I both know who the best doctor is."

I was puzzled. "What do you mean?"

"He's the guy who fixes Jordan up." He looked indecisive for a moment. "If I don't get this right, I'm no damn good. Let's get to work."

Jordan, still in pain, raised her head. "I've had this before with you. I know you're going to get it right, Tom, because I trust you."

Bromley put on a pair of gloves and smiled. "Let's get to work,"

I nodded as he adjusted the bed and stood close to her as the nurse positioned her IV. In the background, the heartbeat of the unborn baby echoed in the delivery room. Tom raised Jordan's gown, exposing her pregnant mid-section. Using his hands, he quickly manipulated her abdomen, pushing on the baby. Perspiration gathered on his forehead, but his hands remained calm as he continued to push. I could tell there was movement because the geometry of her abdomen changed. I also saw the sign of success in his eyes. After a few minutes, he asked for an ultrasound to see the position of the baby. He stared at the image for a moment. But instead of confidence, I saw his brow knit above his surgical mask.

"The umbilical cord is around the baby's neck," he spoke with a raised voice. "It wasn't there before we turned the fetus. Get me the forceps!" he commanded firmly to the nurse.

She handed him two metal instruments that looked like small tennis rackets.

Bromley put the two sides into the birth canal and then gently turned them. "I'm turning the baby's head with forceps," he said.

Slowly the baby's head started to peek out with the blades of the forceps on either side.

"The cord is around the baby's neck. It feels loose, but it may tighten. We've got to get this one out quickly!"

As the baby continued to come out, I could see the snake-like umbilical cord around the baby's neck. As a surgeon I felt helpless; I could only watch.

Bromley remained cool. He put his gloved finger through Jordan's dilated uterus and slipped his finger under the cord. With deliberation, he gradually moved it over the baby's head and pulled it away from the baby's face. I could feel my heart beating faster. Then I looked at Jordan. She was clutching the sides of the table, and the muscles in her neck were strained. I held her hand in mine and took a damp washcloth next to her head to wipe away her perspiration. We still didn't know if it was a boy or a girl.

Suddenly, there was a noise, squeaky at first, and then a loud cry. The baby came out, and Tom held it up. "It's a girl!" he shouted triumphantly.

I looked at Jordan. Her tears of happiness and the smile that spread across my face would stick with me as long as I lived.

Chapter 3

Having a second child in my forties was a challenge for which I was ready. My eight-year-old son, Joey, was a gift I thought I would never have. A terrible first marriage and a near ruination of my career put me on the ropes. Then I met Jordan, and my life changed. While Joey is our joy, we couldn't have another child. It was something about antibody rejection. Then the impossible appeared. The death of a young woman led us to the gift of a fertilized embryo. The miracle worked. By fate, we had the child we both wanted.

It would be a while before I could hold the baby, so I went to the neonatal unit and looked through the window. She seemed so small and fragile as she cried. But, boy, did she have a set of lungs. No wonder. Giving up the comfort of the womb in exchange for the big, bad world would do that to anyone. It wasn't long before she was descended upon by the nurses who cleaned her up and swaddled her.

A few minutes later, another doctor came in with a tray full of swabs, Band-Aids, and needles. He was tall with carrot-red hair dangling below his surgical cap, but because of his surgical mask, I couldn't make much more out of him. He put his tray on a small table next to her bassinet and pulled out a metal instrument that looked like a postage stamp with a sharp point. I stared fixedly at the name tag on his scrub shirt: Dr. Earl Crandall.

I knew what was going to happen and winced as he pushed the sharp needle into the baby's heel. He collected a small amount of blood and put it on a glass slide as my daughter let out a cry. I'm glad Jordan wasn't here to see it. This was all routine for Crandall, but after all this, she was now our daughter. When Crandall finished, he took a cotton swab and rubbed it on the inside of the baby's cheek for DNA. Then he picked up his tray of specimens and walked nonchalantly to the door; he looked like he was ready to dispense his pain on another innocent patient.

I walked out and saw Sennett waiting for me.

"Well, Pops," he said, "how does it feel having a beautiful daughter?"

"Kinda like I get a second chance to fix all the mistakes I made with the first child. Exposing him to Mafia killers is generally looked down upon by the experts." I was about to say something else when Sennett's cellphone started chirping. He pulled it out of his jacket, listened for a moment, and then clicked it off. His gaze turned inward, and his lips pressed slightly as he let out a heavy sigh. I had seen this look before. It usually meant trouble.

"We have a problem, Ben. You need to get your car, and I have to make a stop on the way. I'm sorry. It's because of all the disturbance at the gun rally." In fact, Bromley's voice seemed to lose its power as he shook his head. He quietly said everything was okay and tried downplaying what was going on outside of the hospital. "Just so you know, the stop is at that gun rights rally that started today. Seems as though a white supremist group is involved. Don't worry, the police have it under control."

"You get a couple of days to settle down with Jordan's recovery in the hospital," Bromley said. "I'm figuring I'll hide behind you, and you'll get any problems straightened out."

"No worries," I said.

It turned out that two hours would be plenty of time. Sennett called Sergeant Axel Knudsen to get Sennett's car down to Grand Circus Park. I had heard about the rally, but I really hadn't paid much attention. Gun rights in the city of Detroit were straightforward. You conceal a gun, and you go to jail. In Detroit, at the age of eighteen or up, it is legal to buy a handgun with a purchase license from a private seller who's at least twenty-one. In summary, it is legal to buy a firearm from a federally licensed dealer. No purchase license is required to purchase a muzzle-loader (a firearm that is more than twenty-six inches long) in Michigan.

Sennett said the rally appeared to be an election thing. Jack Kilkearney, a right-wing congressman from Texas, was stirring up hate and fear in Michigan, hoping the voting public would respond to a racist candidate. One thing was for sure—the rally was going to get a lot of coverage. Both the governor and senator faced election, and conservatives were displeased with their performance and what they were seeing.

As we drove down Woodward Avenue toward the renovated downtown of Detroit, there was an increasing presence of police stationed along the way. In the distance, we could see a crowd near Grand Circus Park. Created in the 1860s, the five-acre Grand Circus Park is part of a growing residential area that connects with some of the city's favorite places, like the sports arenas for the Tigers, Lions, and Red Wings. At times the teams have the honor of being the best franchises in the country. It is now a place to sit in the sun on a summer's day next to the fountains and see live theater, hear music, be entertained by street performances, or just people watch.

That wasn't the case today. Encircling the park were hundreds of people holding signs and yelling. Some of them were stripped to the waist, showing off numerous tattoos. Others were dressed in leather pants and shirts with muzzleloading guns and bony horns filled with gun powder. On the other side were hundreds of men and women with signs imploring gun control. Most of them wore some type of head and chest protection and bull horns in their hands. Their message was clear. As we got closer, we edged up to a couple of squad cars and parked next to them.

Sennett got out of the car and walked up to one of the officers, a young guy dressed in protective gear, including a helmet and face mask. A baton was strapped to his waist, and a large shield rested against a police wagon.

"What's up, Jim? You got this under control?" Sennett asked, as he moved forward with his shoulders back and chest out.

"A lotta bullshit, Lieutenant. This guy, Kilkearney, is a real nut job. He's a gun rights loudmouth from the deep South. If you're not white, not a believer of their God, and not in the NRA, you're un-American. Just got to be careful, not do something stupid and set him off," Jim said. "By the way, what happened to your nose?"

Sennett hummed a song and then said, "I fought the law, and the law won." As he spoke, he nodded and scanned the crowd. Across the park, I could hear the protestors yelling something that sounded like German.

"What are they saying?" I asked as my shoulders tightened.

"*Meine Ehre Heisst Treue*," Jim said. "My loyalty is my honor. It comes from World War I and the Waffen SS. Can you believe it? We fought a war to get rid of this shit."

"There's always someone who hates," I said. "They blame someone else for what happens to them. You can't get rid of it."

I was about to say something else, when some pushing and shoving got started by a dozen placard wavers who broke through the ring of police officers. Two of them came running toward us. One had a Mohawk with a shaven head and a tattoo—PENI—engraved on his neck. The look on his face read trouble. I recognized the other; it was Jack Kilkearney. They both gave the impression that they were looking for a fight. I turned to Jim and quietly asked him what the tattoo meant.

Sennett couldn't resist when he saw it. "Public enemy number one. These are some bad people.

Before I had a chance to respond, Mr. Tattoo pushed against Jim and knocked his shield to the ground. I didn't think it was an accident and neither did Jim. Suddenly, Kilkearney and his friend stood in front of us. It wasn't long before several others arrived. Kilkearney stared at me for a moment as if he recognized me. "You're that Jew doctor, aren't you?" As he spoke, he spit on the ground.

I could feel the blood rush to my face and the muscles in my arms tighten. "If I am, it's none of your fucking business. Get it?"

"I read about you, trying to be a detective, solving crimes. What a joke. Maybe you should spend more time being a doc and less time being stupid."

"I don't know what your problem is, but I'm not making it mine." I started to walk away.

Then he stepped in front of me with his face close to mine, close enough I could smell the booze in his breath. As I continued to move, my shoulder hit against his. He used it as an excuse to take a swing at me. I ducked, but his fist hit my chest. There was no choice. I bent over low as my coach had taught me, and I suddenly exploded upward, ramming my fist into his upper abdomen. He went down in a heap.

It didn't take long for a dozen more dudes to run up, yelling, "Jews will not replace us." They were ready to do battle. Jim had picked up his shield and had his baton in his hand. In one fluid motion, he whipped the working end of his stick hard against the front runner's left leg directly on his quad muscle. No sooner did he go down than Jim had cuffed him.

By this time, there were twenty more policemen breaking up the me-lee. I looked for Sennett. He was running up to the crowd with a bull-horn in his hand. He stood in front of them, his face twisted with a fierce anger.

"Okay, jokers, you want trouble? That's dumb. It's a lockdown for all of you. We have about thirty regular cops ready to send your sick asses back to where you came from. You can either back off or look forward to grabbing your ankles at Jackson Prison. What'll it be?" Nobody messed with George Sennett. His voice was carefully controlled as he drew in slow, steady breaths while showing false smiles.

The crowd seemed to hover for a moment with a desire to fight and then slowly melted back onto the street as if they were looking for easier conditions. Bullies are like that.

Kilkearney got up from the ground and brushed off his jacket. He looked at me for a moment. "I'll get you some day. You may not know when, but I'll get you."

I couldn't figure out what this man had to do with me. I'd never met him before, didn't know what his beef was.

"If this is a threat to this man's life, I'll arrest you right now," Sennett snarled.

Kilkearney held up his hand. A crooked smile moved his lips. "No problem. I'm just an honest citizen speaking my mind."

I could see Sennett waiver. He could arrest him, but it also could es-calate the situation. He turned to Jim. "Escort this piece of crap back to his ride. If he gives you any trouble, take him down to headquarters, and we'll deal with him."

When the police pushed Kilkearney into a squad car, the demonstra-tors seemed to lose their mojo and started to disburse. From my stand-point, I wanted to get the hell out of here. My wife had just had a baby; this was no time for confrontation with a bunch of nut jobs. Instead, I looked across the park and saw Knudsen. He was waiting for me with Sennett's ride.

Sennett grabbed my arm and started walking toward Knudsen.

"That was a pretty dumb thing you did. Did you consider you were outnumbered?"

"Well, he hit me, and from my standpoint, they were going to beat the crap out of me, regardless."

"I suppose, but you had the entire police department on your side."

"From my perspective, I wanted to be alive to thank them, especially Jim."

Sennett smiled. He knew this conversation wasn't going anywhere.

It wasn't long before we reached Knudsen. The sergeant was a stolid type. Always efficient, always short on talk. He gave me my keys and then hesitated for a moment. "Better take Jefferson and the expressway. The governor has mobilized the National Guard."

I was taken aback. Knudsen never gave advice without being asked. I thanked him and told Sennett I was headed home to make sure my son, Joey, was okay. I opened the door to my twenty-five-year-old Jeep Wagoneer. I loved my ride. I never was much into material things, but this ungainly hunk of steel and I had been through a lot together. That's why I kept it in good shape.

As I pulled away from City Hospital, I felt it was déjà vu. I pressed my hands to my temples. Detroit had suffered from the Black-White hatred for decades. Now it seemed it was happening again. Just different spewing of hate from different people. I didn't have time for any diversion.

Chapter 4

I HUSTLED OUT OF GRAND CIRCUS PARK through a cordon of cops until I reached my ride and exited onto the expressway. When I returned home, I saw my eight-year-old son, Joey, waiting for me through the window in the kitchen. Dorothy, our sitter, opened the door. She clasped her hands to her chest and had tears in her eyes when I told her we had a girl. She knew what we had gone through to get there.

At first, I wondered how Joey would take to competition in the household. Then I thought of their age difference. Suddenly, I wasn't worried. "How about going to the hospital and seeing Mom?" I asked.

I didn't have to wait for an answer. He already had his jacket on. I thanked Dorothy for staying and then walked with Joey to the garage. Twenty minutes later, we were back at the hospital.

Oddly, Joey didn't say much on the way over until we reached the hospital. Mostly he was staring down at his hands. It wasn't like him. "Dad, can I ask you a question?"

"Sure."

"There's an older kid, Jimmy Granes, at school in the fifth grade. He said something really mean today."

"What happened?"

"It was recess. A bunch of kids were on the playground when he came up to me. He had three or four of his friends with him. He said something like, 'Your dad is a doctor, isn't he?' When I said yes, he said you must not be much of a doctor because you kill people. Then all his friends started laughing and making fun of me."

A schoolyard bully. I could feel the warm blood of anger heating my face. It happened to me when I was a kid, and it still makes me angry. "You remember when that man came into our house and wanted to do something bad to your mom, don't you?"

He nodded. "Did you kill him?

"I did, and I'm not proud of it. But if I didn't, he was going to hurt someone else, including your mom."

"So you saved someone's life? That's like a doctor."

"That's true, Joey, and well, sometimes you have to do things to protect yourself and the people you love. Most of the time, people respect that. But a kid like Jimmy Granes has his own problems. He wants to make himself look bigger by trying to make someone else look bad. It's called bullying. And trust me, there are a lot of bullies around."

"They are still going to make fun of me. And they even yell bad words at my friend Wes."

'What kind of bad words?"

Joey looked down at the sidewalk. "You know, the N-word."

I could feel my teeth clenching and my face redden as I parked the car in the doctors' lot. "There are things your mom and I can do, but you're going to have to help," I said, carefully measuring my words.

He didn't seem to understand.

"Joey, don't give the bully the satisfaction that he can make you feel bad about yourself. Mom and I will speak with the school, but you have to do some things also. Remember you're a good kid. Keep up activities with your friends and play sports. If the kid bothers you, look him in the eye, don't say anything, and walk away. It's going to be hard, but in the end, you're going to win. If it gets out of control, we'll go to the principal and have a talk. Now let's go inside and see Mom and your new sister. After that, I have tickets to see the ball game. Are you interested?"

He nodded his head.

I could tell he was still rumbling over what I had said, so I looked at him and put my hand on his shoulder.

"Dad, when that man was in our house, were you scared?"

"You bet I was, but sometimes we all have to stand up and take care of ourselves and the ones we love."

"I get it. Just like with a bully?"

"You're right." I smiled. "Life is full of bullies, and they come in different forms. Sometimes it's in business, sometimes it's in school, and sometimes it's in sports. You never know when or where you'll find them."

Joey seemed better after our talk. I could tell he was excited by the bounce in his feet. We made our way up to Jordan's room. I told him to wait by the door so he could surprise her.

I peeked around the door and saw Jordan in the bed with our baby. On her head was a small cap, and her eyes were closed as she slept. Next to her was a tall, slender woman in her mid-twenties with freckles and strawberry-blond hair. It was her nurse. The badge read Sally Richards. I silently put my finger to my mouth and then motioned to Jordan to close her eyes. Then I went back outside and went over to Joey.

"Let's go in and surprise Mom," I whispered.

When we got past the door, he shouted out, "Mom!"

At the sound of Joey's voice, she opened her eyes and pretended to be surprised. Then she motioned him to come over to the bed. "Take a look at your sister, Joey."

He looked at her blue eyes with the inquisitiveness of an eight-year-old. Then he cautiously touched her forehead. He seemed enthralled. "What is her name?" he asked.

"Well, your father and I decided to call her Sandra Wells Dailey. What do you think of that?

"That's a funny name. Why don't you call her Blue?" he responded.

"Why?"

"She has blue eyes," he replied.

Jordan looked at me and winked. "What do you think, Ben?"

"Baby Blue. I like it."

"I am so happy," she said with tears exiting from the corner of her eyes.

I understood why. She carried the deep blue eyes from the fertilized embryo of Sandra Wells, a courageous woman who died because she had unraveled a desperate plot to ruin the city's investment in the new medical center. We had both determined that the baby would be named after her.

I told Jordan Joey's story regarding the school bully. She agreed that speaking with her teacher and the principal would be a good idea. What

I didn't tell her was the incident at Grand Circus Park. Right or wrong, I didn't think she needed that kind of stress. After an hour, I could see Joey was getting tired.

"I think you should get going, Ben," Jordan said. "I'm sure Joey will love the game."

We had decided that we couldn't let Joey feel we weren't giving him attention. A Tigers game on a sunny day worked out, so we left for a matinee at Comerica Park. But this wouldn't be just for Joey; good or bad, an afternoon at the ballpark always had a calming effect on me.

Chapter 5

I'm a football guy. I played in college, and though I was never an all-star, I had a great feeling of accomplishment that I stuck it out. I loved the game because of its physical contact, the strategy, and the team coordination it takes to win. But as a fan, I find sports like football, basketball, and ice hockey move so fast that unless you have an instant replay, you miss the nuances of the game. That's why I like baseball. It gives you time to think, see where the players are located, consider where the ball should be hit, analyze how the defense plays against the batter. It's a game you can watch while also having a Coke, eating a hot dog, talking to your kid.

Like today, the Tigers were playing the Red Sox. The game was tied in the eighth inning, and the Tigers had men on second and first. Miguel Cabrera was batting. Cabrera, possibly the best right-hand hitter of his generation, could hit for both power and average. The pitcher was a young kid, getting his first shot at him. I knew Cabrera could throw summer heat, and it didn't take long for the kid to find out for himself. He threw a hundred-mile-an-hour fastball, and Cabrera hit it deep into the centerfield seats.

Joey was standing up and yelling. It probably would be the only time in the game he would get excited today. The Tigers were in last place and probably doomed to be there all year. When he sat down, he looked up at me. "Dad, the scoreboard said that pitch was a hundred and one miles an hour. How did he see it?"

"Everybody has his own special talent. Good baseball players have a gift of hand-eye coordination. They can hit those balls. And just to be sure you know, your dad isn't one of them."

"Yeah, but you're a good doctor. I bet they couldn't do what you do."

"It's like I said, Joey. Everyone has his own special talent."

Amazingly, the Tigers won. By the time we got home, Joey was asleep, and I put him to bed.

A few hours later, I was about to go to bed when my cellphone crackled. It was Sennett.

"Where are you?" he asked.

"Home. What's up?"

"Jordan called me. Your daughter is missing."

"Missing? How can that be?"

"We've got the hospital and the police out to find her. I can't tell you anything else."

Chapter 6

WE WERE AT THE HOSPITAL. SENNETT, who until this time, had remained quiet, got up from his chair and stalked the room. When he got to the end of Jordan's bed, he sat down again.

Randy Templeton, head of the FBI for Detroit, arrived and mentioned some article from the National Center for Missing and Exploited Children that said 47 percent of US infant abductions occur in hospitals. "I understand you haven't spoken with Earl Crandall, who was in charge after the delivery. His records and the people I've spoken to have been exemplary. I'm not inferring anything; I'm just asking a question now. Is there anyone that either of you would consider capable of this?"

Both of us shook our heads. Jordan's family was from Florida. Her mom and dad were thrilled with their daughter's family and her siblings who were happily married, living on the West Coast. My parents lived in a Detroit suburb. After watching their son get married and then have a baby boy, their grandson became the center of their lives.

Sitting in Jordan's room, my mind swirled about how we had gotten another child from an implanted frozen embryo, a gift from a determined young woman, Sandra Wells.

Sandra had been a patient of mine. She had worked for the city as a lawyer. While there she uncovered a multi-million dollar bilking of the city's new hospital by a criminal organization. I remembered her and the conversations we had about my family and my profession. Mostly it had been about being the police surgeon for the city. She had even asked me if I knew anything about frozen embryos and whether I would ever worry about an unborn child. I had told her that my wife and I had had trouble having a child, but from what I knew it was a great success and, if my wife and I had no other option, we would do it. It had been a strange discussion, but she had seemed satisfied with my answer.

Her friends told me that Sandra was the most organized person they had known. Apparently, they were right. She had told them she had a frozen embryo and, if anything happened to her, she had plans for her unborn child. Unknown to Jordan and me, she had legally decided that Jordan and I could be the parents. Sandra must have also known something that would lead to her death.

I thought about her death and the arduous tracking down of the killer and her family. Her parents were dead, and her only surviving relative was her cousin, Charmayne Phillips, who lived in Windsor, Canada, across the river from Detroit. If family members were responsible for most infant abductions from a hospital, Charmayne certainly didn't fit the mold. Yes, she was not married, but I could not conceive she would do something so horrific.

There was also the sperm donor. He was a law student who graduated from the University of Michigan. I remembered his name, Jake, but his real name was Jonathon Edwards. He was in Sandra Wells's class.

I couldn't ignore any possible cause. I turned to Sennett and asked, "What about Charmayne Phillips?"

"I already called Inspector MacGregor and told him we were going to have a chat with her."

I looked over at Jordan. Her eyes had cleared, and there was a determination in her face as the prosecutor in her took over. "Do you really think she did it?" Jordan asked.

"No way," Sennett replied. "But you know the police business, we can't take anything for granted. I've set up a meeting for tomorrow."

After a couple of deep breaths, she said defiantly, "Count me in."

Normally, I'd know there'd be no use in telling her not to go, but this was different. "You're going home tomorrow and rest. There's a limit on how much the body can stand."

Jordan didn't argue with me.

I left Jordan to move my car from the hospital entrance. As I got out of the front seat and stepped onto the pavement, the keys slipped out of my hand. I picked them up and looked up at the other side of the driveway. There, walking on the sidewalk, was a tall man in his late twenties in a scrub suit. At first it was no big deal until I noticed his red hair and quickly made the connection. I slammed the car door and started running after him, yelling, "Hey, you, stop where you are," and rushed toward him.

He must have seen the anger in my face because he took off across the parking lot in his sneakers.

I had on a pair of loafers, but I didn't care. The adrenaline was pumping hard, and I knew there would be no way this guy would get away. Dodging between parked cars, I saw him pull out keys from his pocket. About a hundred feet from me, he opened the car door. I waited until he was just across from me and hit him high at the shoulders and knocked him down. Giving him a closer look, I saw the man was in his mid-twenties. His face was clean shaven, and his red hair went across his forehead. In a weird way, he reminded me of Robert Kennedy. I stood him upright and slammed his back against the car. As I did, I heard him yell for help. In the distance I saw Sennett and two guards running from the front of the emergency entrance.

"What the hell are you doing this for?" the young doctor asked.

"Where's my daughter?" I yelled.

"What do you mean?"

"We're going to find out if you kidnapped my baby from the hospital nursery."

"What baby?"

"The one you kidnapped."

"I don't know who you are, but you're out of your mind. I don't know anything about your daughter. My name is Robert Conklin. I'm a surgery resident at the hospital on the obstetrics service."

I looked at him again. Was he the man I saw taking blood from my daughter? Was he the person who kidnapped her? Now I wasn't so sure. By this time the police had arrived. I relaxed my grip slightly and stared at him. "Where is your badge?"

"I misplaced it. I've got to go to security tomorrow and get a replacement."

Sennett arrived and checked out the young man's credentials. We waited as one of the hospital's executives came down. They called Templeton to sort out the facts. It turned out the red-haired man's name was, in fact, Robert Conklin and, as he said, he was, a third-year resident in the general surgery program. His alibi of being in surgery at the time of the kidnapping was solid. They finally let him go.

No one had gotten hurt, and when I explained what I had done, Robert Conklin thankfully accepted what I said. He had heard about the kidnapping. Nevertheless, I felt stupid and embarrassed. This only increased my anxiety. I needed to have a cool head and not act like some kind of out-of-control cowboy in a Western movie. I walked away with Sennett. Thankfully, he understood.

Sennett looked at me for a moment. "C'mon Ben. Go back to your wife. You need some rest. We're going to see Charmayne Phillips tomorrow."

Chapter 7

I was devastated. No one can begin to explain how they feel about a horrific crime like a kidnapping. It brought both intense anger and a depression of loss that only a parent can feel. On one hand, I wanted to get my hands on the kidnapper and kill him or her. On the other, I would pay anything, give anything to get our daughter back.

Jordan was exhausted from the events that had transpired. She tried to talk, but soon her eyes started to droop, and she dozed off. It wasn't long before I also fell asleep and dreamed about our baby. In my dream, I held her in my arms and smiled at her warm body next to me. In my dream there was no kidnapping, only happiness. When I awoke, it took me a moment to realize it wasn't real.

The afternoon sun was gone. I checked my watch. It was seven o'clock. I rubbed my eyes and looked at Jordan. She stirred from her sleep. Like me, she seemed dazed.

"Did anything serious happen?" she asked desperately.

I shook my head. "No, but we're going to find out something today. George and I are going to meet with Charmayne Phillips. Then we're going to meet with the hospital."

Jordan got into a wheelchair, and the nurse got behind her. In her lap were a Teddy bear from a friend and some cards of congratulations in a plastic bag. I carried her suitcase.

As soon as we reached the elevator, another mother with her baby came up next to us. She looked as if she wanted to say something. When the elevator opened, I told her we were waiting for someone and to go ahead. When the elevator doors closed, Jordan turned her head away so no one could see the tears drifting down her face.

The next elevator was empty, and we went down to the entrance of the hospital. Sennett brought up the car. We must have looked pathetic because, from the expression on his face, I could see he was tearing up too. It was the first time I ever saw him get emotional.

It took us half an hour to get through traffic and reach the house. Jordan remained silent the whole time. I parked the Wagoneer in the driveway where Dorothy was waiting for us. I had told her what had happened and prepared her for what I was going to say to Joey. We made our way inside.

Joey was waiting impatiently. He asked where the baby was. Reluctantly, I told him the baby had to stay at the hospital for a while. When he asked why, I said the doctors had some tests to run. I knew that not telling him the truth would come back to haunt me, but Jordan and I decided to ease him into the reality of the situation.

Shortly after, Sennett arrived. It was a good thing because Joey loved him, especially when he played catch with his football. It didn't take them long to get into the backyard, playing catch with Bucky, our Labrador retriever.

Inside, I helped Jordan to the couch and arranged a couple of pillows. Then I went to the kitchen to get her a glass of water to take the two pills that Tom Bromley had prescribed. Dorothy went with me.

In the kitchen, Dorothy said, "Doctor Dailey, I'm so sorry for what has happened. I don't know what to say. No one prepares you for something like this."

"You're so right, Dorothy." As I spoke, I glanced at my watch. I had a meeting with the hospital employees responsible for my daughter. It was time to leave.

Chapter 8

The last time I saw Charmayne Phillips was in Brian MacGregor's office. We were searching for the killer of Sandra Wells. Charmayne was her only living relative and turned out to be a valuable source of information. She was close to her cousin and deeply upset with her death. Because of her relationship, I thought this was going to be a difficult conversation, but one we had to have one.

Brian MacGregor, chief inspector on the Windsor Police Department, came along with us. He thought it might be wise to meet Charmayne at a neutral place and not at police headquarters.

Sennett, MacGregor, and I met her for lunch at the Treehouse Bar and Grill on Oullette Avenue, Windsor's main drag. It was a modest-looking building about three blocks from the Detroit River. Its claim to fame was the best pizza in Windsor. We arrived early, took a booth near the entrance, and ordered a couple of Cokes.

Charmayne arrived ten minutes later. I recognized her from our previous meeting, but there was a difference: she had glammed up. Her Dutch boy hair style was now long and swept to the side of her face, and she was thinner. We stood up when she walked in and waved her over to the table. One thing hadn't changed: her handshake was firm. Cutting to the chase, she asked why we wanted to meet with her.

Sennett replied first and told her that her cousin's child had been kidnapped.

A look of terror filled her face. "Why? How can this happen?" she said as she squeezed her eyes shut.

Just as she finished, the waitress came over. At this point food wasn't an issue. Charmayne asked for some tea.

"That's why we're here," Sennett said. "Do you have any idea why this might have happened?"

"You don't think I had anything to do with it, do you? It's bad enough that my cousin was murdered by that awful man."

The waitress returned with her drink.

MacGregor interjected. "We don't know who was responsible, but we're going to call anyone who might have had some contact with this situation. The police are not accusing anyone. We thought you might have some information that could be useful."

Charmayne bit the inside of her lip as she sat pensively for a moment, staring at her teacup. "Sandy was such a beautiful person. She so wanted a family. She was also the most organized person I ever knew. That's why she made Dr. Dailey the custodian of her embryo."

"Is there anything you would consider of interest related to your cousin?"

"Nothing that I know of. Nobody knew about the embryo, including me."

"That leaves Jonathon Edwards and Thomas Carlyle as the only other people that knew about the embryo. Carlyle is the lawyer who drew up the papers for the IVF for us."

"Did you know Jake Edwards?" Charmayne asked.

"I met him once. He seemed like a really nice guy. Quiet and very smart. At one point, I thought he and Sandy would get together. But I never knew about the embryo."

I asked her if she knew where he practiced. She said he was with the city of Detroit legal aid. He was a civil rights lawyer.

"How did you find out about the embryo?"

"It was known that she was going to have an embryo baby. She sent her friends and me an email that a baby was going to be born from an embryo. Apparently, the attorney who worked out the details for the birth was under orders from Sandra to notify me if there was a baby born from the embryo." Charmayne began to rubbing her wrists.

"What did you say? You must have been shocked," Sennett said.

"At first, I was a little hurt that she never said anything to me about making Dr. Dailey and his wife the guardians of her embryo. She was a very private person. I think she didn't want to put a burden on me. I got over it, and I miss her terribly. In a way, with the birth of the baby, I feel Sandy didn't really die."

"Just to clear the air," I said, "she never knew Jordan and I would be the parents. Initially we were merely the guardians."

"Did you have any contact with Thomas Carlyle?" Sennett said.

"Not personally," Charmayne said, "but I did look him up on the internet. I'm a nosey kind of person. I like to know everything. When I heard about the embryo, I checked his background. He had a good reputation with adoption placement. From what I read, he is very active in family law and the right-to-life movement. There were a couple of websites and even a blog. I read one of them."

"What did it say?"

"He's hardcore, especially when he got into the evangelical point of view on abortion. It made a woman who aborts sound like a murderess."

Sennett, who had remained silent, seemed to be deciding what to say. "I have to ask you this, Charmayne. Can you tell me where you were yesterday?"

"You don't think I had anything to do with the baby's abduction, do you?"

"No, but if I don't ask the question, I'm not doing my job."

She explained that she was at work yesterday and had people who would vouch for her. I think she understood. It was clear there wasn't much to talk about. I was ready to get up when I thought of something.

"You know, Charmayne, I just realized that you, my wife, my son, and I are now related. The baby is your niece. So you're now part of the family. Is that okay with you?"

"I would love to be part of your family. I will do anything I can to help find the baby. I could see the tears as she dabbed her face with a handkerchief and stared down at her empty hand.

"Well, you should know the baby has a name," I said. "It's Sandra Wells Dailey."

It's strange that a person can switch so quickly from being happy and to being sad. I had a hard time believing there was any way she was involved with the kidnapping. After she left, Sennett and I stayed to talk with MacGregor. By the time we finished, we both decided it was doubtful that Charmayne was involved. Regardless, MacGregor said he would check out her alibi.

At the same time, it was disappointing that we were no further ahead.

I turned to Sennett. "You've read the Declaration of Independence. Right?"

"Yeah," he replied. "Why?"

"It says all men are created equal. They have unalienable rights of life, liberty, and the pursuit of happiness. Obviously, the framers weren't talking about women. What's your opinion about abortion?"

"It's really a woman's choice. She's carrying the baby. I mean what if it was incest or rape? How can you force someone to have a baby she never wanted? I'd let the mother make the decision. It's her life, her body."

I got in Sennett's car, and he drove me home. It was a silent drive as I rested my head on my hand. There was nothing left. I was filled with an intense emptiness at the loss of my child and an overwhelming anxiety about Jordan. I was planning to do something.

Sennett must have known how I felt because he told me they were going to do everything they could do to find the baby. "Follow the clues" was what he said. I knew he was trying to help, but I didn't need a pep talk. I was like a caged animal. I would not stop until I found her. He read me and said he'd give me a few moments with Jordan and then join me in the house. I didn't object.

Jordan had heard me arrive and greeted me at the door. We sat on the couch in the living room, and I held her hand. In return, she put her head on my shoulder. There were no tears, just a deep breath as if she was clearing her head. I told her about my meeting with Sennett and Charmayne.

"I am so depressed, Ben. These past nine months, the thought of a baby was all I cared about. Now she is gone."

"I understand," I said, trying to console her. "But we are going to find her. Trust me. I am not going to let up until we find the baby."

Jordan nodded her head as if she knew the drill. Ordinarily, what I said would have been empty superfluous words, but we had a history together. At this point she might have even believed me. It was what she wanted to hear.

"Do you think there is a chance?"

"I swear to you. I will find her." That's all I said, but it must have made Jordan put her prosecutor hat on.

"How?"

"Follow the clues. That's what George told me."

After our discussion, I sat in the kitchen staring out at my backyard and trying to sort out what had happened at the hospital. I was certain that I had seen Conklin in the nursery. But as to whether he was the kidnapper, I was no longer was sure. Frankly, I was worried that I was losing my self-control. So was Jordan. That's probably why I appreciated Sennett now sitting in the chair across from me, as I stood solidly and tightened my fists.

"Ben, we must stay disciplined," he said. "I understand how you and Jordan feel, but it will do no good to lash out at suspected people. That's the job of the police."

As he spoke, I looked down at the floor, as if it would give me guidance. Nothing appeared, so I just nodded. "You know me, George. I'm clenching my jaw and grinding my teeth."

Sennett nodded his head slowly, as if he was remembering our past. We had a mutual bond from intense life-and-death experiences. That's why I had a police badge and why he listened to me.

"Yes, I do know you, but I can't imagine how I would feel if this would happen to me," he said.

"I need to be proactive. I need to be on the hunt for the bastard that did this."

"You're right," Sennet said. "And so do I. The problem is we must be correct."

I turned around and saw Jordan walking into the kitchen. "Maybe the kidnapper realizes he or she made a mistake," she said, "and the baby will be returned.

It was so sad to see how beaten Jordan was. I knew her purpose was right, but reality sucks, and we couldn't solve this ourselves. We needed help.

George pulled a small notebook out of his shirt pocket and leafed through it. After a few moments, he put it back and leaned forward from his chair, facing Jordan. "I know Doc and I know you. You both have the credentials to help in this search."

It was a relief that he would ask me to help. I felt like someone had taken off the load on my shoulders. Sitting still was not an option, but I needed the authorization. "Where do we go from here?" I asked. "About the embryo, Thomas Carlyle, Charmayne Phillips, Carlyle's secretary, and Jonathon Edwards? Regarding Carlyle, Charmayne mentioned he was involved in the right-to-life movement and family law. Beyond his legal business, I don't know what that means. As far as his secretary is concerned, she is new to the job and appears to have known only the fact that Sandra Wells gave you and Jordan the embryo."

"Maybe we should look into Carlyle's business," Jordan interjected. "The secretary mentioned that he had a blog following."

"I'll put that on the list," Sennett replied. "There has to be an answer."

Just as he finished talking, his cellphone buzzed. As he picked up and listened, I saw his furrowed brow and his hand clenched on the phone. He mumbled a goodbye and put the phone back in his pocket. "That was the police lab. Guess what they found in the dust in the floor in the nursery."

I shook my head.

"Gun powder," he said.

"What the hell," I stammered. "What does that mean?"

"I wish I knew. Strange that it would coincide with the pro-gun rights demonstration. We have some work to do. It's going to start with Thomas Carlyle."

CHAPTER 9

I DROVE TO MEET WITH SENNETT AT Thomas Carlyle's office at the Penobscot Building the next morning after I dropped Joey off at school. On the way over, I was almost ready to tell Sennett that I needed to stay with Jordan rather than see Carlyle. But after all we had gone through, I owed him. More than that, I knew Jordan wanted me to go and do it for Sandra Wells. It was her gift that changed our life.

I parked my Wagoneer on the street and walked into the lobby of the third tallest building in Detroit. As I passed through the art deco entrance, I immediately encountered Corrado Parducci's Native American sculptures. I looked at them for a moment, long enough to feel the grip of a strong hand on my shoulder.

Turning around quickly, I saw Sennett facing me. He had his work face on—stolid, creased eyebrows, and pinched lips that made his face angry. We got into the elevator and exited at the forty-fifth floor. As soon as we got off, I recognized the name on the door in front of us—Thomas Carlyle, Attorney at Law.

After entering the outer waiting room, we encountered his secretary. The sign on her desk said Alice Vanderveer. We had called ahead, and she was expecting us, so she took us into his office. It was in a corner of the building, facing southwest and giving a panoramic view downriver past Grosse Isle toward the mouth of Lake Erie.

Sitting behind his desk, Thomas Carlyle wore a starched white shirt, regimental blue-and-red tie, and a pinstriped gray suit. Attached on the corner of his lapel was a pair of small white feet. He had a look of genuine concern. His head was tilted back and with his gaze looking up. He was the same imperious man that Jordan and I had met to read Sandra Wells's will. It was that moment that changed our lives, as we accepted the privilege of caring for Sandra Wells's frozen embryo. Rising from his seat, Carlyle came around his desk to us.

I introduced Sennett.

Carlyle's eyebrows rose. "What is it I can do for the police department?"

"You may or may not know," Sennett said, "but Dr. Dailey and his wife had their child kidnapped from City Hospital. We're talking to anyone who might have had some relationship to the child. You were the attorney associated with the transfer of the embryo. That doesn't mean you did anything wrong, but you might let us know something we should look at."

Carlyle returned to his desk and took a newspaper off it. "I read about your newborn baby," he said. "I am terribly sorry."

I nodded as he stared at the floor. "We wondered whether there may have been some phone call, letter, or contact that might have some relationship to the kidnapping," I said.

Carlyle looked around his office with a slack expression and wet, dull eyes. He must have noticed that the door was open because he closed it and went back to sit in his chair. "Sorry, my secretary has this habit of never closing the door." He paused for a moment and then continued. "After I had the meeting to give you the right to have Sandra Wells's embryo, I haven't heard or seen anything except what I saw on the news." He reached for his reading glasses on the table and then picked up a file. He looked through it and came out with a paper. "Before you came here, I pulled out our file just to see if there was anything there that might be helpful." When he finished looking at it, he handed me a copy.

For a second time, I read over the document that he had drafted for Sandra Wells. I knew what it said. Months ago, when we had left his office, Jordan and I had read it over a dozen times. When I was done, I handed it to Sennett.

He had seen it also. "Who has access to this document?" he asked.

"Really no one but me," Carlyle replied. "It's in our computer data bank. We scan and file the cases. If they are interesting, I may keep the originals. This was certainly one of them."

"What about Jonathon Edwards?" Sennett asked. "He's the young man who donated his sperm for the embryo. Has he ever contacted you?"

"No, never heard from him. I understand that's not unusual in cases like this. Occasionally, we get someone who is looking for money, but that wasn't the case here."

It was clear there was nothing more to gain from talking to Carlyle, so we thanked him and got up to leave. He again said how sorry he was over the kidnapping. When we reached the door, he asked if we would close it shut.

Sennett and I walked through the waiting room toward the exit and were just about to leave when Carlyle's secretary called out to us. We stopped near the door. She paused, as if uncertain whether to speak. I wanted to encourage her so asked if anyone had mentioned the case to her since we adopted the embryo.

"You know," she began, "I've been working here for a while, but I still don't know all the people that come and go. But there was a gentleman that came to the office for a meeting with Mr. Carlyle. Unfortunately, he was called into court and couldn't meet with the man, who then became upset. He wanted to talk to Mr. Carlyle about the Wells's case. He had come a long way to see him."

"What more did he say?" Sennett asked.

"He asked if I knew anything about the Sandra Wells case. I didn't give him any information and told Mr. Carlyle about it. He asked me if the individual left a card or a call back number. He didn't leave anything, and I never saw him again."

"Does that happen often?" Sennett asked.

"Not often. I'm new here. Funny you should ask me that. Mr. Carlyle does family law and works with a right-to-life organization. He actually has a blog called *Save the Child*. A lot of people come and go to his office related to that. The ones I've met are wonderful caring people. I think it is just wonderful what Mr. Carlyle does, keeping the unborn alive."

"Were there ever any problems that you know of about the Sandra Wells case?"

"None that I know of," she said. Then she stopped, contemplating. "You know there was one thing that happened about a year ago. There was a break-in at one of the in vitro fertilization clinics at the hospital where they store the embryos."

I nodded my head. "Since we had an embryo in the hospital, we were told that a generator failed and some of the refrigeration stopped. Some embryos were lost as I remember, but they said it had nothing to do with our child."

Alice was about to say something else when Carlyle came out from his office with some paper in his hand. For a moment, he seemed surprised that we were still here. Then he returned to his secretary. "I need to get this document out today."

We took that as our cue to leave and thanked them for their time. Carlyle was silent as we made our way to the elevator. When we got to the car, I got behind the wheel, put the key in, turned on the air conditioning, and stared out of the window. "What do we have from all this?" I asked Sennett.

"We have a kidnapped child, a man who wanted to talk about the Wells's case, and an attorney who is a right-to-lifer with a right-to-life blog."

The uncertainty was making me anxious. "What do we do now?" I asked.

"We have to find Jonathon Edwards. In the meantime, we need to talk with the hospital and the individuals who took care of your daughter."

Jordan and I had wanted our names on the list as parents of the embryo as noted on the delivery of the child. Thomas Carlyle had completed the proper legal paper for us. Since Jake Edwards was on the list for the embryo, he had asked if Tony Reynolds could be on the list. Jake had agreed that if there were any problems with the parentage, Jordan and I had first legal control of the embryo after the child was born. Carlyle had had Jordan and me sign a document that would prevent any claims.

CHAPTER 10

THE HOSPITAL PERSONNEL MET US THAT afternoon. Mostly we talked with nurses who had contact with delivery, went over nurses' notes and times when there was contact, and viewed a TV in the neonatal area. All checked out as routine care. Nothing appeared that was significant. I was told by the nurses that the only other person who had contact with our child was Earl Crandall, the doctor responsible for embryo fertilization at City Hospital. His job included following up on the delivery and making sure the DNA and other blood tests were taken properly. The results were still pending, but there did not appear to be any problems.

When we met Crandall, my first thought was wondering if he had passed puberty, he looked that young. However, once we started talking, he appeared to be straightforward and knowledgeable. He claimed that since the baby was from a fertilized embryo, he took special swabs for DNA and blood tests across the hall from the nursery. Once he finished, he said he took the baby back to the nursery and signed a note on the chart stating that the baby was returned. This was also signed by the nurse on duty. From there he left to go back to his office on the sixth floor. Crandall seemed helpful but had no answers as to the abduction. Just to be sure I asked for the records of other nurses for their signature when my baby was moved. They were all signed.

I had a text message but found it annoying to find a phone number on the message I had never seen. Then I saw a photo, and my hands started shaking and my stomach contracted. It was my daughter in the blanket she was wrapped in when I'd last seen her. Below it was a text message: "I've got her now. If you try to find her, bad things will happen." I showed Sennett the text.

Within minutes, he was on the phone, speaking with the police lab to find out where the call came from. He made it clear that this was urgent. It took thirty minutes to find out. "The phone belonging to Cathy McNamara is here," he said. "I've got my guys on it."

I paced back and forth, stopping to look out the window. By this time, two squad cars had arrived.

"Who the hell is she?" I asked.

"She's a seventeen-year-old girl from Birmingham, Michigan. They called her out of class. It turns out she lost her phone at a shopping mall yesterday. She didn't report it lost. We checked on it with Verizon. As far as what the text said, this girl was talking about playing the volleyball game that afternoon."

I called Jordan while we searched for an answer. When she heard the news, she became animated. "At least from the tone of the message, I would think that Baby Blue is alive."

"It sounds that way," Sennett interjected as he shifted from one foot to the other. It was a ray of hope, but the location of the text could mean anything. We tried the "Find My Phone Option. It was dead."

"We've talked to two of the people that knew Sandra Wells, Thomas Carlyle, and Charmayne Phillips," Sennett said. "That leaves one other person—Jake Edwards."

Sennett's secret weapon was Knudsen. When it came to law enforcement, especially something like a kidnapping, Knudsen could negotiate through any bureaucratic spider web. It took him about a half an hour to send to Jordan's computer a list of Sandra Wells's graduating class. There were 212 names.

She printed up three copies of the list and gave one each to Sennett and me. I looked at it three times. So did Sennett and Jordan. There was no Jonathon Edwards. When I asked why, I was told he had graduated a year before.

"Sandra Wells was a very careful person," said Jordan. "What if she didn't want anyone to know the name of the donor? It could be a different name and Jonathon Edwards was an alias."

"How would we find that person?"

"We have a cellphone and a list. Let's start calling. Let's use Martindale and Hubbell again to find them." This is a book with all of the practicing attorneys in the country. It took three hours before we finished the list. The task was frustrating. A number of the names were no longer practicing at the firms listed in the Martindale list. However, when we did reach someone, we mentioned that this call was related to a kidnapping. At that point, they were very helpful. Several of the contacts knew Sandra Wells and spoke highly of her. She apparently had a lot of friends. We made a list of them, especially the ones that were repeated.

"We need to find a better way," Jordan said. "Why don't we call the law school again and see if we can make some sense out of all of this."

Sennett got hold of a woman at the admissions office. When we explained our problem, we were told that, as a general policy, the school does not give out information on their students. When he told her it was associated with a recent kidnapping, she suggested we speak to the academic dean of the law school.

The dean, Frances Robertson, answered after the first ring. After explaining our problem and mentioning the death of Sandra Wells, she became interested. "I knew Sandra very well. What a tragedy," she said with a heavy sigh.

"Do you recall a friend of hers in law school named Jonathon Edwards?" Sennett asked.

Robertson told us that before she could give any information, she would need a letter from the Detroit Police Department and then an acknowledgement from the school that she could send us information. An hour later, she called back and suggested a meeting tomorrow. When Sennett told her about the kidnapping, she arranged a meeting that afternoon.

Sennett and I arrived at the ivy-clad buildings of the law school in the afternoon. Frances Robertson's office was on the second floor with a panoramic view of the central campus. To many visitors, it was a structure similar to those found in the Ivy League.

Robertson welcomed us in and said, "As I recall, Sandra had a few friends, including me. But the one person she hung around the most with was Jonathon Edwards. I remember that everyone who knew him called him Jake."

We repeated the name several times, wrote it down and thanked her.

She looked him up and found his name in Detroit. He was now a legal aid defender in Wayne County for the city of Detroit. "Jake was an interesting character," she added with a satisfied smile. "I looked up his bona fides. He graduated summa cum laude, law review, Order of the Coif, and the Lambda Law Society."

"I assume that's not bad for a law student," Sennett said.

"The only thing better is a Supreme Court clerk. He applied, but it was his personal life that ruined his chance."

"What do you mean?"

"It was his intense desire to change the world. He never could stand the status quo. Pushing the envelope of the law. He got arrested a couple of times for disorderly conduct associated with gay rights."

"How was he in school? With all his awards, his professors must have loved him."

"Not really. His professors frequently came to me telling me how argumentative and disruptive he was. From what I heard, he was a loner, loved the out-of-doors, and didn't hang out with his classmates, that is, except Sandra Wells."

"Was he gay?" Sennett asked

"I don't think so. Women seemed to be attracted to him, and he returned the favor. Like I said, he seemed to be an advocate for gay rights. That doesn't mean he's gay. For him, it was a crusade. He was vocal about it and got arrested during a protest. I think he did it on purpose to start a dialogue."

"Was Sandra Wells one of his attractions?" Sennet asked.

"As far as I know, they were just friends. Sandra came to me after graduation. She told me she took a job at the mayor's office in Detroit. It was strange, but she wanted to speak with me about Jake. It was personal stuff, like she was getting serious with him. I had to be careful about what I said and warned her about his record of problems with the police."

"What was her response?"

"When I told her what it was about, she didn't seem to care. She said she had a friend who wanted a sperm donor for an embryo. It was weird. You'd think she would talk to a doctor first."

For some reason, to me, it seemed odd that he was a public defender. Not being an expert on law schools, I expected that most law students with his achievements would get a position in a big firm with a big salary and big prestige. That wouldn't be a public defender. Then I thought of Jordan; she has similar qualifications, and she works as a federal prosecutor. It made me chide myself for being so mercenary.

There wasn't much left to discuss with Robertson. We were about to leave when Sennett asked if there was a picture of Edwards.

"Sure, we have photos of all our students." She opened up her computer, and after a couple of minutes, she showed us a picture of a young man with sandy-brown hair, a strong jaw, and bright eyes that seemed to stare at us through the computer screen as if he knew who we were. I took a photo with my phone.

"Nice-looking, clean-cut young man," I interjected. "Just the kind of lawyer I would want if I was in trouble."

"That's what a lot of people said about him. Too bad he got into trouble."

"Why? Defending the rights of people is the essence of being a lawyer, isn't it?" I said.

"That's true," she said, "but those high-paying, big lawyers don't look at it that way. They want these students to march in lockstep with the firm. Some stay, and some can't stand the pressure. I'll tell you one thing. Jake Edwards doesn't back down from anyone.

"What do you mean?"

"If he wants his justice, he'll get it. He has his own ideas of right and wrong. Even if it required something physical, he would do it to get what he wants. He has a short fuse. Eventually, it is going to get him in trouble."

We thanked her and made our way back to the car. Sennett got behind the wheel, stared. out the window for few moments, and then turned on the ignition. "Don't be taken by how he looks," he told me. "The serial killer John Norman Collins looked like a choir boy."

"That's true, but Sandra Wells was nobody's fool. From what I know, if she picked Edwards to be the sperm donor of her embryo, she vetted him well."

Sennett nodded. "Just remember what Templeton said. For everything concerned, he's our best suspect."

Ten minutes later, Sennett had Edwards's secretary on his speaker phone. Sennett told her who he was and that he wanted to talk with Mr. Edwards. He didn't tell her why but said it was police business. They made an appointment for an hour later.

We entered the building of his office and took the elevator to the fifth floor. The sign on the door read Jonathon Edwards, Community Law. On entering the office, we saw three men in dirty overalls and angry faces. No sooner than we opened the door, a blond-hair, young woman, probably in her early thirties, came up to the counter at the front of the office. She motioned to us to follow her.

Walking toward the counter, one of the men shouted, "What about us? We've been waiting here for over an hour."

"I'm sorry, but you'll have to wait," she responded. "Mr. Edwards is running late."

Cracking his knuckles, the tallest of the men yelled, "I got a hundred-dollar fine for parking my truck on the street, and I have to wait for this guy who hasn't shown up for a meeting? Who the hell does he think he is?" He looked threatening.

Sennett turned to the man who spoke. "Settle down. The lady told you all she knows."

"You're telling me to settle down. Who the hell are you?" By this time, he was out of his chair and made his way toward Sennett.

"Well, to begin with I'm a police officer. I don't know what your problem is, but you're threatening this lady. Now back off."

"Bullshit! I'll tell you what I'll do. How about I meet you outside, and I'll kick the shit out of you." I was close enough to him to smell the booze from his breath.

"If you're looking for trouble, you've found it," Sennett said calmly. "Threatening a policeman is a crime. Now you have a choice—go to jail or walk out of here and make another appointment, perhaps with a different lawyer." As he talked, he showed them his badge and his holstered SIG Sauer.

The power of alcohol wasn't enough to keep the man challenging Sennett. He looked at his two friends, shrugged his shoulders, and they all walked out.

Sennett looked at the young lady. She didn't seem upset.

"Are you the gentlemen from the Detroit Police Department who called earlier?" she asked as we walked back to Edwards's office.

"We are," Sennett said and introduced himself and me.

"Don't worry about them. They just wanted to hear the results from Mr. Edwards. They parked in a tow-away zone and didn't like the idea of getting a ticket. Mr. Edwards settled it with the court."

As she studied our licenses, I looked around at his office. In contrast to its dinginess, his desk was neat with three folders in the corner, an organized desk set, and a PC on a computer stand. Under the circumstances, I guessed I probably would have had an office like this. It had no frills, except for a large photograph above his desk—untrammeled forests and a quiet lake with an island in the middle. In front of the backdrop was a tall young man, probably in his twenties. Next to him was a yellow canvas canoe. I recognized it. "Nice country," I said. "Looks a lot like the Algonquin in Canada."

"You're right," she replied, a little surprised. "He always talked about canoeing there. Now how can I help you?"

"I thought I recognized it. I spent a lot of time in the summer there when I was a kid," I said. "Our being here is a long story that I think we should discuss only with Mr. Edwards."

"Yes, but he hasn't been here for the last week. He was supposed to be here today, but he called in this morning and said he wouldn't be in."

"Did he say why or indicate where he was?"

"No, but he did sound a little funny. Like he was talking to me but thinking of something else. He said to cancel his appointments for the next week and have his cases cancelled."

"Is he sick?"

"He mentioned he was under the weather. You know, a cold or something like that."

There wasn't much more for us to discuss, so we thanked her. As we were walking out, Sennett asked her to stay in touch if Edwards called back.

When we exited the building, I told Sennett that I was sure the picture was from the Algonquin Provincial Park in Canada,

"How did you know?"

"There is something about the park that is unique, especially my experience with a canoe."

"I'm all ears."

"I was just a kid when I first went there. It is the source of one of my worst camping adventures. I was starting medical school, and I knew I would never have another chance for free time, so on a whim, I decided to go camping in the Algonquin Provincial Park in Ontario. It's one of the largest canoeing grounds in North America. I registered with the park ranger, took my canoe off from my car, and set off. While I was there, I got caught in a freak snowstorm in late August. I had to break into a forest ranger's cabin and hunkered down for a few days. When I returned to my car, I was in a rush to go back to Ann Arbor. I didn't think much about it, but I was in such a hurry I forgot to tell the park ranger I had come back. It must have scared him when I didn't show up because they sent one of the largest rescue searches in the history of the park to find me. They called my mother to tell them I was missing. When she told them I was back in school, they were a little less than happy. Needless to say, they didn't invite me back."

I paused for a moment and then got serious. "George, I am wrought up. Honestly, I want to get my hands on the person who did this. I've never been a violent person, but I can't imagine anyone doing this to us."

Sennett interjected. "Can you think of anyone who would be involved in this plot? Was there any conflict? Is there anyone who wants to get even with you? Has anyone contacted you in any way regarding the embryo?"

"Not that I know of. As far as I know, nobody knows. I'm not involved."

"Do you think anyone else knew about the child?"

"The only person that knew about it was Thomas Carlyle, the attorney. Sandra Wells drafted a document that if he ever let information get out that this child was related to Wells, he would be guilty of a criminal act that would cause him to lose his legal license and cost him millions of dollars to say nothing about a jail sentence. He signed it. As far as anyone else knows, it was an implanted fertilized egg and the donor is unknown."

Sennett looked distracted. "I hated camping," he said, staring at the photograph on his phone. "I don't like sleeping in tents, not taking a bath, and crapping in the woods."

"I'm surprised," I said. "Even a city boy can get used to it."

"You know, Doc, there is always something new about you."

I thought about my kidnapped daughter. "Sometimes I wish there wasn't."

"What did you think about Edwards?" Sennett asked.

"It's coincidence he's not in his office. He never misses a meeting is what his secretary said. Right now, he is a prime suspect. We have circulated his photo to the newspapers, television, and radio."

I told him I came to the same conclusion.

Sennett's phone buzzed. It was Templeton. He listened for a moment and then clicked off. "The lab guy just called. They analyzed the powder they found on the floor of the nursery. It's pyrodex, a granular powder designed for use in front-loading muzzle rifles and black powder cartridge arms."

My mind flashed back to the demonstrators in Grand Circus Park.

"It doesn't take a rocket scientist to assume that the police should implicate the gun rights demonstrators," Sennett said. "The only problem is there were two or three hundred people there."

"All we have to do is find the one with red hair and gun powder on his shoes," I said.

"We can do it. The department was worried about some kind of disturbance, so they took videos of the demonstration. Let's go home and look them over. In the meantime, we must find Edwards."

CHAPTER 11

We talked with Templeton about Jake Edwards not showing up. He immediately verified that Edwards was suspect number one. He was going to get his "wanted name" spread over the country and put his face on the television. In the meantime, we came to the conclusion that we had to review the videos from the gun rights protest in Detroit. It was going to be an onerous task to go over a twenty-four-hour demonstration. I didn't care, and neither did Sennett.

I called Jordan to update her, and she said she would look at videos. While she sounded good, I knew the telephone doesn't always reveal what you discover with just listening in person. Although Sennett and I were beat, we knew we were not going to dissuade Jordan. She was a federal attorney and handled some tough cases. We stopped at a deli, bought sandwiches and a salad for Jordan.

When we got home, Jordan was on the internet trying to find more details on Jake Edwards. That lasted for another twenty minutes while I put out dinner. Joey and Jordan joined us. We tried to make things seem normal, but Joey was quiet, which was unlike him. Kids understand more than what we give them credit for.

As soon as Jordan finished, she asked about the video. Sennett said it was on a website at the police department. Five minutes later, he had it up on Jordan's computer.

While we continued to eat, I watched Jordan. She went to the computer and opened the video.

"Are you going to be on that screen for a while, Jordan?" Sennett said.

She nodded and kept staring at the screen while Sennett and I ate. After fifteen minutes, she excitedly called out. "Look at this!"

We both jumped up and went over to her computer. There on the screen was a man who looked like he was in his late twenties or early thirties. He was medium in height and dressed like a mountain man with a coonskin hat. Around his neck was a muzzleloading rifle. However, the one thing that stood out was his carrot-red hair, flowing out from beneath his hat.

"Can you make a copy of that on your computer, Jordan?" Sennett asked.

"Sure." Within a couple of minutes, she had isolated the man on the screen and saved the picture.

Sennett wasted no time. He called Templeton and had Jordan send the photo to him.

"They're going to take this photo and put it in the Free Press for tomorrow. This is huge to have the photo. If we're wrong, who knows."

I felt like we were doing something positive, but the anxiety of losing my daughter continued an emptiness I couldn't get rid of, and the more I thought about it, the angrier I got. There was one good point. Jordan was active and in the hunt. Finding this man was a start.

It didn't take long for the pictures to come out in the newspapers and television, along with an Amber Alert in the Detroit area. To top it off, a rash of people popped up, stating they had seen the stolen child. But none of them produced any solid leads. Jordan stayed home with Joey while studying the internet for a clue. It was a tedious procedure. There must have been a hundred call-ins. After a couple of hours, we had checked out all the calls. At the end of the day, a woman named Alice Carpenter from Cadillac, Michigan, contacted us. She was sure she knew the man from the hospital. His name was Chris Winkler.

The next morning, I joined Sennett in his office. He knew Cadillac from his days at the police academy. He also still knew Dean Frazier, now the Sherriff of Wexford County, which includes the city of Cadillac. Sennett phoned him. After a few pleasantries, Sennett asked him if he had ever come in contact with Winkler. Apparently, he had, along with his arrest record. Sennett put the call to Sheriff Frazier on speaker phone.

"What can you tell me?" Sennett asked.

"I don't know what happened to Chris. I've known him since he was a youngster. He was a good kid. When he finished high school, he joined the army and worked at a field hospital in Iraq. I know one thing; when he came back from the war, he was changed. They said he had posttraumatic stress syndrome. He could never find himself, going from one job to another. I remember he worked construction when he could; otherwise he did odd jobs and lived in a shack on the outskirts of town. We've arrested him a couple of times for disorderly conduct. Chris liked his booze."

Sennett replied, "We had him identified in a video during that gun rights demonstration. There was a kidnapping of a newborn child, and he was identified as a possible suspect."

After a moment of silence, the sheriff responded. "You could never tell with Chris. He was a big gun rights person. You know the kind, a pickup truck with rifles in the back window and a Confederate flag that he would put on his truck on the Fourth. But then, he has the right, and he did serve in the army and had an honorable discharge."

"What about Cadillac?" Sennett said. "I checked it out. There was a swastika affair a couple of years ago that caught the attention of the press. Then there was this gun rights thing, something about a gun rights sanctuary in Wexford County."

"We've got our problems, George. You know, it's a never-ending battle."

"Dean, I need you to check out Winkler's house as soon as you can."

"I'm out of here right now. As soon as I get there, I'll call you."

It was agony waiting. Sennett felt it too as he walked back and forth in his office. Templeton was the coolest, but I wondered how he would feel if it was his daughter.

Exactly a half-hour went by, and then the phone rang. Sennett picked it up and put it back on speakerphone.

"George, there's trouble here. I can feel it. Winkler isn't here, but there are diapers and nursing bottles. A baby was in this room. His truck is gone. The only thing I found was a scrap of paper with a phone number."

"Who owns the phone number?" Sennett asked.

"We're not sure. It had a North Dakota area code, but it turned out the number was out of use. By the way, we found something weird in

Winkler's garbage can. It was a burnt-out book. The best we can make out of it was from the Colchester Collection."

"What's that?" Sennett asked.

"We're not sure," I said. "I asked Knudsen to check it out. It's a collection of the Holocaust."

Frazier said, "I know the book. It's filled with writings about the Holocaust, the Jews, and antisemitism."

Sennett said, "We need to alert the state police and the FBI."

"I'm on it," Frazier replied. "The idea that someone kidnapped a baby makes my skin crawl. I don't know how long ago the child was here, but we're going to try to throw a net around this."

Before Sennett left, he called the Detroit FBI offices and spoke to Templeton. Frazier seemed to be satisfied with the conversation. When Sennett finished, he picked up a packed bag that he stored for this kind of situation. Then he called Knudsen.

"George Sennett told me you're my contact downtown," Knudsen said to the sergeant.

"I need you to have your gun and a backup just in case," Sennett said. "Write down the numbers before we leave, and give a copy to the doc here. I've also left a few numbers for you to call if necessary, including a woman named Alicia. We're going to be riding in the doc's car back to Detroit. Here's Dailey's license plate. The doc will give you his driver's license. Make a copy."

Knudsen followed the orders. As we walked out of the building and put Sennett's gear in the Wagoneer, he asked me if I had a spare key. I told him there was a magnetic key box under the front fender and showed it to him. He asked me to lock the door because he wanted both of us to walk down the block. I found out the reason when we got to the corner. There was the yogurt shop. I walked in and was greeted by Sennett's girlfriend, Alicia. She gave me a hug and then turned to Sennett. I think she knew there was some trouble.

"Ben, you look very serious. Is everything okay?"

"We have a problem, Alicia," Sennett said. "I can't see you tonight. We're going out of town."

"Do you want to tell me about it?" she asked, sounding disappointed.

"Something bad happened to the doc and his wife. Their newborn baby was kidnapped, I'm going to help him."

Suddenly skin bunched around Alicia's eyes, and she stared painfully and listened intently as Sennett explained what had happened. "That explains everything," she said. "About two weeks ago, a nice-looking guy came in and started talking to me. He said he knew you and the doc. He said he was so happy about Jordan's pregnancy." She stopped for a moment, as if she realized what she said. Suddenly, she started crying. "I should never had told him what you told me, that she was going to deliver any day."

"It's not your fault, Alicia. How would you know?"

Sennett waited for a moment and pulled out his cellphone. "I want to show you a photo." He pulled his phone out of his jacket and went to his pictures. After a couple of minutes, he saw what he wanted and showed the photo to Alicia.

Her face exploded with excitement. "That's him!"

Sennett turned to show me. It was a picture of Jake Edward. The realization made my heart race and my anger rise. I now knew the kidnapper.

"Doc and I are going to find him." Sennett contemplated and then said, "As I said, we are going out of town for a few days. I just wanted to tell you how much I love you. That's so if some other guy tries to take my place." Sennett smiled.

Alicia came up to him and put her arms around Sennett's neck. "You're my man, Georgie. I understand your job. Just stay in touch if you can."

"I will. I promise. Right now, we're going to Cadillac, but I don't know where we will be from there."

I saw fear in her eyes, and she looked at me. "Doc, this isn't your first rodeo with George. Take care of him."

"Georgie and I are on it," I said as I nudged Sennett with my elbow.

Sennett looked at me. He knew what I was thinking. "It's just a name, Doc. No big deal."

I laughed. "Sure, George, I understand. I've got to go home and talk this over with Jordan. I'm not sure how she will take this idea of going to Cadillac.

WHEN I REACHED HOME, JORDAN WAS sitting in the kitchen, staring out the window. My mother was with her.

Jordan was holding a cup of coffee and didn't seem to see me. "Why are you home this early?" she asked. "I thought you were going to meet with George."

"I did meet with him. That's why I came home. We have a lead on a potential suspect in Cadillac, Michigan."

Her eyebrows rose when I said it. "Well, something is better than nothing. What are you going to do?"

I hesitated for a moment. "I want to go with Sennett, but my first thought is about you. You need support, and I feel guilty leaving you alone."

Jordan looked up at me. "I know you, Ben. If you don't go, you will never forgive yourself. If you're worried about me, I'm okay. We'll make it through this together. Just stay in touch with me. I don't want to worry about where you are."

It was what I expected. "Are you sure? This isn't about me; it's about our family."

"I know. I'll hold things together here. You've got a cellphone. Stay in touch with me every hour. If I don't hear from you, I'll call you directly."

"How long before you call me?"

"I'm thinking of calling you every hour. Unless you call me and say you're okay, I won't smother you. Is that all right with you?"

I nodded my head.

CHAPTER 12

Cadillac is the geographic center of the lower peninsula of Michigan, about a three-hour drive from Detroit and an hour from Traverse City. Sennett told Templeton what happened and that we were going up to Cadillac. Templeton said he was needed to hold down the fort in Detroit and would be ready for whatever happens. He gave Sennett an FBI agent in the area to call if he needed.

At home, I sagged against the door and reached out to stable myself. Then, I gathered a few things and stuffed them in a bag. I felt like hell when I got into the squad car with Sennett. I knew if I didn't find my daughter, I could never live with myself. Sennett quickly checked out his night bag and then called his captain. He told his captain what he was doing and got a verbal OK. A letter of authorization from the FBI would be on it tomorrow. He also got one for me. We were officially on the case.

We reached the Cadillac Police Headquarters around one o'clock. It was in a modern brick building on the northern end of Lake Cadillac. When we entered, Dean Frazier was waiting for us. He was a fire plug—short and muscular—with a squad cut and a ruddy face, probably from growing up in the Michigan out-of-doors. Sennett introduced me, but Frazier acted like there was no time for chit-chat.

"George, we sent out an all-points bulletin, along with the license plates on Winkler's truck. We just got a call a few minutes ago from a camper. The truck was found near the Old Indian Trail. We gotta get going."

We hustled out to Frazier's SUV and headed north of Cadillac on US-131, following the Old Indian Trail, which was the main track for the Odawa going north to Traverse City. It was discovered over a period of years and is now a historic trail. We slowed down as the trail turned north and joined M-37 to the stretch at what is now called Chums Corners. Its biggest draw is outdoor activities and the nearness to the Interlochen Music Camp.

Our car followed Highway 137 and then right on US-31. It was getting late in the afternoon, but just as we made the turn, we saw a soft dirt road heading into the woods. Sennett parked his SUV at the side of the road and started walking down the rutted path. The dirt was soft and stuck to our shoes. As we walked, we came upon a truck with the tail end in a ditch. When we got there, Frazier said there was nobody in the truck or the ditch.

After walking down, the road a hundred yards, Frazier stopped and looked down at the ground. "There's blood on the ground," he said.

We walked a little further and saw a state police car at the edge of some woods. After a few minutes, an officer saw us and came toward us. Frazier identified him as Sergeant John Thompson. They greeted each other and then walked into the edge of the woods. There on the rutted road was a body propped up against the trunk of a tree. The greyish face and the twisted mouth were repulsive. At the bottom of the tree was a dark circle, almost as if was painted.

After looking at him, Frazier turned back to us. "It's Chris Winkler. Shot in the head."

"What do you make of that dark circle?" Sennett said.

Frazier looked annoyed. "Just sap from the tree," he replied. That's all he said. He seemed more interested in speaking with the deputy.

"Why are you here?" Frazier asked the deputy.

"We got a call and came out. What do you know?"

Frazier told him there was a kidnapping and the dead man looked like he was involved. The baby had not been found. Thompson said there was nothing in the truck to suggest a baby.

Frazier went to the truck and opened the door. Then he bent down on the carpet on the passenger side. He put his nose close to the floor.

"Man, I'd recognize that smell anywhere. My kid had it. It's the formula they feed infants."

I was stunned, realizing that my daughter had probably been there. The realization was almost too hard to bear. "How long do you think he's been here?" I asked.

"There is no evidence of rigor mortis; that usually comes after three to six hours," Sennett said. "Insect and maggots are usually there ten to fifteen hours."

"So someone has my daughter, and it's been at the most six hours."

"We did find a map in the car. It wasn't marked out, but it was folded, showing mostly Montana, Wyoming, and North Dakota."

"What does that mean?" I asked.

"I think we should take a look at that burned-out truck. No criticism of the FBI, but everyone misses something."

We went to the side of the truck, and as we did, a policeman got out of his car and came up to us. His name tag read Jared Brown.

"This is a potential crime scene," he said. "What are you guys here for?"

Sennett showed him his Detroit badge and handed him the letter from the FBI. When Brown was done, he gave Sennett back the letter. "What do you need? The FBI told the chief that you would be coming here."

"We just want to look at the truck. I'm sure there was nothing left untouched, but it's my job," Sennett said. Before he started, he called the special agent and got the okay to examine the vehicle.

The truck was a mess. Sennett pulled out a flashlight from his bag and got down on his knees to look under the truck. I looked with him. There was nothing except burnt metal. As he shined the light to the rear fender of the truck, there was a glint of reflection off the ground.

"What's that?" I asked.

"What?" he asked.

"There's something on the ground that flashed when you shined the light to the back."

The sun was shining onto the rear of the truck, and Sennett didn't see it. So he gave me the flashlight. I pointed it in the direction where I had seen the flash. It flashed again. I got up and went to the rear of the truck. This time, I slid under the fender with the flashlight and saw a metal object that looked like a butterfly paperclip. "George, there's a metal clip on the ground. Do you want me to get it?"

He said to wait, retrieved a needle nose plier from the car and then gave it to me. I reached under the fender and got the metal clip.

"Don't touch it with your hands, Ben."

I opened the passenger door and set it on the front seat. Looking at it closely, it wasn't a paper clip, but it looked like one. I decided to take a photo of it with my cell phone. When I finished, I showed it to Frazier. He got a plastic evidence bag from his squad car, and I gave it to the state policeman.

"How did you find that?" Frazier asked. "I saw those FBI guys go over the truck from front to back. They didn't miss a thing, except for that."

"Luck," Sennett said. "I didn't see it either. It was the way the sun was shining and the doc's position that let him spot it."

"Dean, do you think this is a diversion? The baby could be going in a different direction while we're trying to figure out what's going on here."

"That's going to be tough," Frazier said. "Who knows what kind of vehicle we're looking for?"

"There was a second set of tire tracks on the road coming up to the woods," Sennett said. "They were from dual tires, so it must be a pickup."

"That's a start," Frazier said. "We need to notify the TV and newspapers. Notify all units that there is a pickup with dual tires possibly carrying a baby and put out roadblocks on major roads. We need to do it now. It's getting late. Anyone who has this baby is going to want to get out of Michigan in a hurry."

Thompson didn't wait. He called the office in Cadillac, and within minutes, the word was out. All the major roads, both north to Canada and south to Indiana, were under surveillance. Time was of the essence.

Another state police car and a van arrived. The forensic team went over the area, looking for evidence. When they were done, they put Winkler in a body bag and left for the morgue in Traverse City.

There wasn't much we could do at this point. Frazier drove us back to Cadillac to get our wheels. I called Jordan, told her what had happened, and then said I was coming home. She seemed relieved when I said it.

When I finished, Sennett and I got back in the SUV and headed back to Cadillac. Frazier dropped us off at the station. We thanked him and headed back to Detroit.

IT WAS TWO O'CLOCK WHEN SENNETT'S cellphone buzzed in the car. He answered and said, "Are you sure?" When he got the answer, he ended the call. "All the major roads from Michigan to Canada and Indiana and Ohio have been checked to see if they can find your child. So far, five trucks with dual tires have been stopped. None of them had any evidence of a baby."

I shrugged my shoulders in defiance. "Well, there are only so many points that lead out of the state. You can't cover them all, but if you kidnapped a child, you would think you would be in a hurry and take the main roads."

"That or you decide to swim across the lake," Sennett said.

"What did you just say?" I asked.

"Swim across the lake. It was a joke."

I stopped talking for a moment. "I think you may have something. There is a way to get out of state in a car without driving."

"How?"

"The SS *Badger*. It's a car ferry from Ludington, Michigan, to Manitowoc, Wisconsin."

"How do you know?"

"My parents took me on it when I was a kid. Ludington is a small town on the west coast of Michigan north of Grand Rapids. The ship has been in operation since the fifties and makes the crossing twice a day in the season."

It didn't take long before Sennett got hold of Margaret Timmons of the SS *Badger* company in Ludington. I listened to her on Sennett's speaker phone as he asked if a pickup truck with dual rear wheels had made the crossing. He explained that there was a kidnapping, and he was calling her for information.

"I'm looking at the manifest, Lieutenant. There was a Ford 150 with a Michigan license plate that got on for the 7 a.m. departure this morning. Would you like the license plate?"

"Sure," Sennett said.

I wrote it down as I listened.

He asked Ms. Timmons, the owner, "Does the manifest give any addresses or destinations? Did the driver use a credit card?"

"No addresses, no destinations, and no cards. Whoever was driving the truck paid cash." She must have suddenly realized what was happening because her voice became agitated. "Do you think this is about that baby that was kidnapped?" she asked.

Sennett told her it might be and asked her to call if she came up with any other information. When he finished, he thanked her and slipped the phone back in his coat just in time for it to ring again. It was Templeton. Sennett listened intently and then clicked it off.

"Are they looking for the pickup?" I asked.

"Templeton said he talked to a worker at the dock and asked him if he saw a couple with a young baby. He said there was a man with a pickup truck, a young baby, and a woman. He said it must have been the mother."

"Did he say where they were going, who they looked like, identification?" I asked.

"Evidently, they didn't talk much," Sennett said.

He was going to say more, but his phone buzzed. He checked the ID and picked up immediately. It was Timmons. Sennett put her on speaker phone. She'd remembered a bit more, described the woman as slender, with reddish blond hair. On the manifest, she gave the name of Mary Richards. Timmons said the man with Richards was her husband. Timmons remembered the man had a beard. When she heard about the kidnapping on the news, she called the FBI. They sent an agent to the boat with photos to see if they could make a match. She said it could have been the man with the beard, but she wasn't sure. In the FBI photo, there was no beard. Although she thought there was something in the photo that was similar, she couldn't make it out."

"Did they indicate where they were going?" Sennett asked.

"They were heading west to visit their family with their newborn child," said Timmons.

"Was it a boy or a girl?"

"I couldn't tell for sure. The baby was swathed and in a basket, so I couldn't see it, but there was pink ribbon, so I assume it was a girl," Timmons said.

"What about a license plate?"

The boat company takes down the license plate on all vehicles on the boat, and Timmons gave it to Sennett. She said she didn't have any more information for them, but if she thought of anything, she'd call again.

Sennett checked out the license plate. It was a dead end—a stolen plate from a guy in Detroit.

There wasn't much more to tell, but I decided to call Jordan again. "Well, we have something going." I told her what the FBI found, especially the conversation with the boat company. The drop of hope that our baby was alive seemed to enervate her. She said she couldn't sit by and do nothing. She had an idea to check out some things, something about looking up a blog.

Chapter 13

It was now in the hands of the FBI. I was frustrated and depressed. There was an unknown suspect out there with my daughter and no way to find him. By this time, Sennett and I were on I-96 heading back to Detroit. We both knew we were up against too many missing facts. We were also tired and hungry, so Sennett stopped at a Burger King. I was going to order a Whopper, but I was shamed into a Beyond Burger when Sennett ordered before me. Nothing like a health nut. After the meal and two cups of coffee, we were back in the car, both tired, in spite of the caffeine effect that kicked in after a couple of minutes.

After a few minutes on the road, Jordan called. This time it was about Thomas Carlyle. She found out he was more than just a lawyer. He also had a pro-life blog, called *Lifer Right to Life*. She sent it to me and then said she had to cut the call short but would phone back in a few minutes.

I looked at the blog. Occasionally, the blogs were accompanied with a photo. Most of them related to babies he saved. Apparently, he must have thought it was good for business. The blogs were hard to read, primarily because they discussed only one side of the abortion issue. Along with them were quotations from the Bible, statements from prominent anti-abortionists, and comments on *Roe v. Wade*. Occasionally, there were photos of babies that had been recommended for abortion and now had grown to be young adults. Along with them were their accomplishments. It was tedious, one-sided reading. There was not a single reference to the rights of a woman. In one of the blogs, there was a photo of him with two adults and a young man. Carlyle was standing next to the young man in hunting gear and looking at a deer they must have killed.

Sennett looked at the photo, and a couple of minutes later, the text arrived. He is not a patient man; the most I ever knew him to wait was fifteen minutes. Then he called Knudsen to find out who else was in the photo. Sennett stared at the photo and nodded as Knudsen spoke. When he clicked off, he said, "That's Jack Kilkearney, the congressman from Kentucky that you had trouble with. Knudsen said the other man is Anthony Reynolds, a congressman from Grand Rapids, Michigan. He fits in well with Kilkearney. They both stand for the same ideology—no abortion, extensive gun rights, and what is probably racism." Sennett let out a long breath and then continued, "The third man matched the photo of Jake Edwards."

George is my best friend, but over the years we had never talked about his experiences with racism, but given the characters we were dealing with, I felt I should respond to his overly long breath; it seemed to have a lot of feeling behind it. "I can't say I know what it's like to live in your shoes."

"You can't."

"You know to me that the color of your skin is insignificant," I said.

"You're right, but don't think I got away free of tormenting. I went to a high school where there were only two Jewish kids in my graduating class, Danny Porter and me. Outside of my GPA, the only thing I had going for me at school was sports. It's the great equalizer. Still, during football practice, some kid would make a Jewish slur. The next I knew I was duking it out with him.

"What did the coaches do?"

"They thought it was just a practice thing. I never complained."

"How did they lay off of you?"

"I worked harder than any of them. Then I caught the winning touchdown for the state championship. Nobody messed with me after that. Even if I had their respect, it didn't make it right. What about you?"

"When you're Black, it can hurt, especially at a white school. Before I went, my parents gave me the talk. Thank God they knew the right thing. But it was never good enough. Luckily, I now know right from wrong. Like when I played a football game, and I'd see some of the fans cheering for the Black guy that scored a touchdown for their team, I knew in the real world of those people cheering us on, many wouldn't let us have equality. They only cared about the game. I know who I am. I'm nobody's fool."

I didn't say anything. For Sennett, it was something he faced every day. Although not at the same level, I had the same feeling as a Jew. I'm certain it was not as painful as Sennett's experiences—the riots in Detroit, the unspoken racial slurs as a cop, and not having the same rights as every other citizen of this country.

As I stared at a photo of Chris Winkler, I changed the conversation. "It could be. It's strange, George. Two people I never met that were involved with the fertilized embryo and now I am trying to re-identify them from a hunting photo."

"Yeah, then there is Chris Winkler, who may have kidnapped your daughter. Of course, there is your daughter and now Thomas Carlyle. Now Jack Kilkearney turns up. I don't believe in coincidence. Why is Jake Edwards in that photo?"

"What are you getting at? I don't know who they are."

"The people involved in this are you, Jordan, your daughter, Jonathon Edwards, and Thomas Carlyle. Sandra Wells is dead. I'm betting somehow someone is going to find Edwards, and it's not going to be pretty."

Just then, my phone buzzed, and it was Jordan calling back.

"Did you check out the blog?" she asked. But before I could answer, Jordan asked, "What will we do?"

Sennett replied, "Two things—find Reynolds and Edwards and follow your daughter's trail."

"Wasn't the FBI on this?" she asked. "I assumed they would have interviewed any possible witnesses."

"Jordan, I know this is about our daughter and we're both frustrated, but we have to follow the evidence."

"Ben, we have to do better than that," she said.

I saw Sennett look at me and nod his head.

While we were going back, Sennett got a call from Templeton. They found a Ford F-150 with dual tires in northern Wisconsin. It was burnt out on a rural road outside of Manitowoc where the ferry docked. The truck was burned to the ground. According to the agent, there was nothing to see. The FBI went over the car and got the VIN and the number on the engine block. They traced the license plate and found it was the stolen truck on the ferry to Wisconsin. The truck had been reported missing three days ago by the owner.

"Templeton is a good guy, very thorough. He said he was going to send me a picture of something they found at the scene. In the meantime, we're going to head back to Detroit."

After we got into the car he got into the details from Templeton.

"Why did he call back?" I asked.

"He knows the story and wants to help as much as he can."

It was eight o'clock by the time we returned to Detroit. Both of us were exhausted. When I walked in the door of my home, Jordan saw my fatigue.

"You need to get some rest, Ben. This is going to be a hard thing to follow, and we need to be on our guard."

"I will. It's hard. How are you doing?"

"I never dreamed about going through something like this. But I know we'll find our baby. We have to."

Tears touched the top of her cheek and rolled down. As I held her close, she clutched on to me; I could feel her heart beating fast.

"I am not a quitter," I said. "We'll find her." I wondered to myself whether she really believed me.

Chapter 14

Nothing changed by the following morning. Jordan, Sennett, and I met with Templeton at his office. He didn't seem like your average TV FBI agent. He was medium height, thin, wearing glasses, and not particularly muscular. When he spoke, however, he got your attention, and you'd better be listening. "Who are the people who knew there was an embryo? Who knows it was implanted?" he asked.

"The mother died a tragic death; the father is a public defender in Detroit," I said. I mentioned Jake Edwards in Detroit. "Right now, we don't know where he is. He signed off any rights to the embryo and appeared to be legitimate. In fact, on the legal document of the embryo, the name of the donor is incorrect."

Templeton looked confused. "That's strange. We called his office yesterday and tried to contact Edwards, but his office said he hadn't come in for a couple of days. For him, it was very strange. Right now, he is our best lead as a person of interest. We have a national search going on. So far nothing."

"Do you think he was there when they destroyed the truck?" I asked.

"Possibly," Templeton said. "But we would have to have proof. Again, who knew about the embryo?"

"You'd better write this down," I said. "My wife and I; Sandra Wells, now deceased, and her cousin Charmayne Phillips; Jake Edwards; Thomas Carlyle, the attorney who drew up the legal documents; and his secretary, Alice Vanderveer."

When Templeton finished writing, I continued. "Sandra Wells died, and Jake Edwards is missing. Not very good to be part of this embryo implantation. At least we can assume that the child is alive," I said.

"My bet is that she is alive and probably well," Templeton said. "Didn't they say there were a woman and a man on the boat with her? Our best bet is to start with Jake Edwards. What do you know about him?"

"He grew up in Grand Rapids," I said, "was valedictorian of his high school class, went to Stanford undergrad and the University of Michigan for law school. Not married, no children. Other than that, he seems to have been on a pretty straight path."

"We need to find out everything about this family," Templeton said. "They are the only lead we have to find him." Templeton said he would call it in while we were talking.

When he finished the call, Sennett still had questions. "There is one other thing. We found out about a year ago there was a power breakdown in the facility holding the fertilized embryos. Sandra Wells's embryo was saved."

"I don't know what that means," Templeton said.

"I know, but we must look at everything we have. Maybe there is a relationship." Sennett was about to get up, and then he stopped. "Carlyle has a blog with a photo of himself, a gun rights guy named Kilkearney. Maybe you could find out who he is."

"I know a James Kilkearney," Sennett said. "I had a run-in with him at the gun rights march the other day. The other guy, Anthony Reynolds, is from Grand Rapids and is a congressman in DC. There was nothing on him—conservative, no wants or warrants, upstanding in his community."

Then he said there was something else.

I flinched. I found out early in my acquaintance with Sergeant Axel Knudsen that when you sent him on a job, he was like a dog on a bone. When you asked him to check out something, he took pride in going deep. Such was the case with the fertility clinic holding Sandra Wells's embryo. He told me he checked out the frozen embryo—our child—and told me that the fertilized eggs were stored in liquid nitrogen. Even though I knew how it worked, he proceeded to reassure me. When he was in discovery mode, ultimately you had to wait and listen, even if you already knew. He described the two methods to freeze eggs and embryos are slow freezing, which happens gradually, or vitrification, which happens more quickly. Tanks are essentially a giant thermos that holds a liquid in this case, liquid nitrogen, in a very insulated container without being cold on the outside. Since nitrogen boils at room temperature, maintaining insulation is important. Theoretically, there is a two-hundred-year limit on the frozen embryos.

What I didn't suspect was that he knew of the incidence of shutdowns of fertility clinics. The first case was at Moccasin Bend Fertility Center in Tennessee where five hundred patients lost 1,500 eggs at a university facility. That same weekend, the Rocky Mountain IVF facility in Denver also suffered a malfunction. In both cases, there was a loss of liquid nitrogen. There was a similar event at Southeast Michigan, and by three o'clock, it was not the only shutdown. By mid-afternoon, he had a folder of clinics where the liquid nitrogen had failed. At the time, Jordan and I were notified that our embryo was safe.

The police department investigated the incidents. Pro-life organizations were looked at as the culprits as they railed against random destruction of unused embryos since not all the embryos get implanted, and many are destroyed. They claimed that these embryos had rights and should not be destroyed because they are potential human beings and/or because they believe that life begins at conception. The Church of England, Methodists, the Roman Catholic Church, and many Evangelical churches shared this opinion. However, in spite of the investigations, no definitive evidence was supplied. The incidents are believed to be unrelated. No one was in the clinic overnight when the alarm sounded. The exact reason why the tanks failed was never discovered.

Six months later, the tanks in Detroit malfunctioned. There was a mechanical fire that shut down the machines. Two people died, but fortunately, power was restored and most of the embryos were saved. With a court order, Knudsen found out the names of the families of the survived embryos. Sandra Wells's embryo was among the group. A short time later, the embryo was implanted. Then Jordan delivered our child. The cause of the fire was investigated. The guy that supervised the department was Earl Crandall. At the time, he claimed it was due to a malfunctioning circuit breaker. Again, there was no direct evidence that the embryos were destroyed by some organized protest group.

When I told Sennett the breakdowns, he looked perplexed. "Common things happen commonly. I don't believe in accidental coincidence. I told

Knudsen to investigate the details. Some of these right-to-life groups are difficult to deal with. What I don't like is the fact that Edwards hasn't shown up at his office."

Sennett said their initial investigation on Edwards was benign. "He is an only child. His father is deceased, and the mother lives alone outside of Detroit. I tried calling her but got no answer. Jake Edwards was liked by his fellow workers, was an avid tennis player, and loved jazz music. He's supposed to be pretty good with the saxophone. Apparently, he sat in sometimes with your friend, Sid."

When he mentioned Sid Blanton, I thought that might be a pretty good place to start. Sid owned the Pipeline, a jazz place down by the river. I used to be the intermission man on the piano. That was when I was down and out and didn't have a family. The Pipeline was the place for jazz in Detroit, so good it was written up in the *Times*. A lot of famous people played there. Definitely not me, but it featured talent as good as you get west of New York and east of San Francisco. Nobody pays attention to the intermission guy."

I checked in with Jordan to see how she was doing. There was less angst in her voice, but the sadness was still there. I told her where we were and said I would be home after I saw Sid. Sennett and I drove over to the Pipeline.

Sid was Sid; he never changed. He was just cool—grey slacks, polished cordovan loafers, and an open-collared, blue silk shirt. In his hand was his Calicchio trumpet, and behind him was the trio. They were playing Miles Davis's "So What." There would never be another Miles, but Sid was close. Even Charley behind the bar stopped to listen.

When Sid finished, he put his horn down and came over to us. He pointed to a table near the window. As we sat down, he motioned Charley to bring a couple of Labatts.

I shook my head. "Sorry, not drinking today, Sid. That was a nice solo," I said.

"Jazz ain't for everybody, but those who like it, they are stuck forever. What's this about not drinking? You sick? And you brought the lieutenant with you. I didn't know the lieutenant was on this beat. What's going on?" Knowing me, he must have figured trouble.

"George? He likes all kinds of music. I actually took him to hear Beethoven's Ninth Symphony. He's never been the same."

Sid's eyebrows went up. "Beethoven's Ninth, huh? All men go as brothers. It's the greatest symphony ever composed. I'm impressed."

"The doc here told me you had a wide range of music in you," Sennett said. Then he turned serious. "But we're not here to talk music. I assume you heard what happened to Ben."

Sid's face stiffened. He knew my history. "If it's on the TV or in the papers, I don't listen. Too much bad stuff going on. What's happened? You ain't been here for a while. I figured it was because Jordan was going to deliver that baby."

Sennett told the story. The further he got into it, the more Sid's lips tightened, and he started to crack his knuckles. It didn't get better after Sennett told him of the kidnapping.

"You must have figured that I can help in some way. What can I do?"

"I understand there is a guy who sits in named Jake Edwards. Do you know him?"

"Sure do. He's filled in a couple of times. He plays like Colman Hawkins. Very smooth. He's a nice guy. Apparently, he was well known in the gay community."

"Any friends that you know of?"

"You better ask Charley. He gets all the news here."

Charley was an ex–Navy Seal who spent some time in Iraq and Afghanistan. Burned out by the military, he returned to Detroit and tried to get rid of his demons.

When things quieted down, we went to the bar and started asking some questions.

"What do you need, Doc?"

I explained what had happened to my daughter. A frown crossed his face. I think if I had asked him, he would have put the uniform back on.

"Edwards seemed like a good guy. A lot of his friends would come here when he was sitting in. I couldn't tell you anyone specifically, except for a guy named Vince. I heard them talking one night about a bar in Highland Park called JoJo's."

That information didn't sound like it would do us much good. We were about to leave when Knudsen called. Sennett had his phone on speaker, and we listened.

"Just to be sure," Knudsen said, "I checked out the incident with the mechanical shutdown on the embryos. As you know, Sandra Wells's embryo was one of the affected cases. Apparently, in all the chaos, they rushed the embryos into another container. They said that the Wells embryo was missing for a short period of time. I spoke to one of the managers of the embryo program. Her name is Carol Dundee, a social worker who acted as a liaison between the doctors and the parents. She said most of the embryos were intact. There was nothing you don't know."

"Still a dead end," Sennett said.

"Not exactly. She said that after the incident was under control, a man who identified himself as the sperm donor, named Jake Edwards, showed up. He said he was worried that the embryo was the target. He claimed he had evidence and was going to do something about it. She said she thought he was a nut bag and didn't say anything until she heard about the kidnapping.

I looked at Sennett for a moment and then told her, "We were notified. They said we had nothing to worry about. I checked it out with our obstetrician, and he concurred. We didn't think anything more of it."

Sennett nodded, and after ending the call, he said, "We have to trust them. As far as I can see, they were right. Your daughter was born healthy. Right now, we need to find Jake Edwards."

Five minutes later we were on our way to Highland Park.

Chapter 15

Highland Park is one of two downtown cities surrounded by the metropolitan Detroit area. It originated in the late 1900s and was never incorporated into the city of Detroit. It has the honor of being one of two cities next to Highland Park; the other is Hamtramck, one of the poorest cities in the country. As the city of Detroit deteriorated, so did Highland Park, but its individuality remained. When the resurgence of Detroit developed, Highland Park didn't benefit. A high crime rate, poor police protection, and marginal education opportunities continue to haunt the city's future. Hamtramck also has one of the most active gay communities in the Metropolitan Detroit area. We needed to find Vince.

It was early in the afternoon when Sennett and I walked into Jojo's. The building was an unpretentious standalone building on Woodward near Cortland. There were two cars in the parking area. Next to them were two Harleys. For all intents and purposes, it didn't look much different from the hundred other buildings on Woodward that faced remodeling or demolition.

We walked into a dark interior, illuminated by colored fluorescent lighting that shone off a large mirror behind the bar. In front of the mirror were ten rows of bottles carrying almost every type of booze available. There was also a dance floor in front of the bar and several tables and chairs on the other side. Two men were dancing to Sam Smith's "How

Do You Sleep?" Two tables were taken by four other men. At one of the tables, two men were engaged in a conversation. The couple at the other table were in motorcycle gear, sipping beer and watching the dancers.

Behind the bar was a middle-aged man with a high widow's peak, small eyes, and a large body hidden by a stripped blue shirt with a red bowtie. As we got closer, I saw his sleeves rolled up exposing a tattoo of a star on his forearm, matched by a flat top, shaved close on the sides.

Sennett walked up to him. As he did, he pulled out his badge and showed it to him. "I'm Lieutenant Sennett. We're looking for someone named Vince."

The man didn't seem fazed. "That would be me. What do you want?"

"Do you know Jake Edwards?"

"Sure do. He comes down here once in a while. What do you want with Jake?"

"There's been a kidnapping. We want to speak with him."

Vince's eyebrows moved upward. "That wouldn't be Jake. He is one of the nicest guys around here. You know he's a lawyer. He's helped a lot of the guys that come down here."

"Who are the people he hangs out with here?"

"There aren't too many. He's quiet and usually keeps to himself. I know he has a friend that lives with him over in Palmer Woods. The guy's name is Russell Barnes."

"Anyone around here know him?"

"Sure, those two guys at the table over there both know him well."

We walked over to the table where they were sitting. One was on the pudgy side with horn-rimmed glasses, and the other looked more like a body builder with a tight polo shirt and bulging muscles pushing out the short sleeves. When Sennett pulled out his badge, they looked a little frightened.

"Don't worry," Sennett said. "We're looking for Jake Edwards. Vince over there said you might know."

The heavy-set man spoke first and said he hadn't seen Jake for a couple of weeks. The body builder said Jake told him he was going to see his family.

"Did he say where they are?"

"No, I've known Jake for a long time. He never spoke much about his family. I guess there's some kind of problem."

"Did he ever say anything about a woman named Sandra Wells?"

He thought over the question. "The only time I ever saw him upset was a year or so ago. He mentioned that there was a woman he knew who worked at the city hall who died in a drug house."

"Do you remember the name of the woman?" Sennett asked.

The man shook his head. "Jake is a close-to-the-vest kind of guy. He never talked much about personal things. One thing always caught me about him. His family was a big part of his life."

While we were talking, one of the motorcycle guys started calling out loudly to the two men on the dance floor. "Hey, chief, you like dancing with a man? Make you feel good?"

There was no response, so the other guy at table shouted out to them. "Hey, don't you like pussy? Or maybe you are one." They were laughing uncontrollably. It was clear that the motorcycle boys had had too much alcohol and not enough brains.

Neither of the dancers said a word, but Vince came out from behind the bar. He walked over to the table.

"I think you boys had better get your asses out of here. We don't take customers like you."

"Oh yeah? Tell you what, faggot man. I got a chain here that'll turn your balls into marbles, huh?"

Sennett had heard enough. He stood up from his chair and moved over to their table. "How about you two boys get your sick asses out of here or there will be some trouble."

The smaller of the two men jumped out of his chair and came over to Sennett. "Who the fuck are you? Another one of these rear enders?"

"Okay, Mr. Hotshot. What if I told you I'm a cop and I can put you in jail?"

"You ain't got shit," he said, slurring his words. Then, he slowly moved toward Sennett and pulled a chain out of his pocket. "But I got something here that'll make you very unhappy."

As he pulled it out, Sennett stepped forward and made two quick moves—a kick into his groin and spinning him around in a reverse choke hold.

As the man dropped to the floor, the other man stepped back from the table.

Sennett didn't wait for introductions. He pulled out his badge and pushed the man back into his seat. "I'm going to get you two a free ride to the precinct. Attacking a Detroit Police officer is a serious crime. Any move you make you're going to pay." He took out his cell and called for a backup. In the meantime, the two men went back to the table and slumped their heads down. Within five minutes, I could hear the sirens. Ten minutes later, the two men were in the back of a squad car.

When they left, Sennett turned to me. "We've got to talk to Edwards's roommate."

He called Knudsen and got Edwards's address and his phone number. Ten minutes later, we were in Sennett's car driving to Palmer Woods. The Woods aren't far from Jojo's. Once there, we drove through rows of beautiful old homes reflecting the old line of the richest neighborhood in Detroit. In the area, there were two golf courses near each other, a walking park, and a beautiful pond that becomes a popular ice-skating rink in the winter. I knew the pond well. When I was a kid, I spent hours trying to hone my skating skills. I soon realized that, while Detroit was the home of Gordie Howe, I was never going to make the big time.

Jake Edwards's home was on a quiet, tree-lined side street a block away from the park. I know it could be said that they don't make old-money houses like this anymore, but they don't. Sennett parked the car in front of a 1920s Tudor style home.

We walked up the sidewalk and tapped the brass knocker on the front door. After a couple of minutes, the door was opened by a clean-shaven man, probably in his mid-thirties. I assumed it was Russell Barnes. He looked like an advertisement for Brooks Brothers, red checked shirt with the cuffs rolled up, tan pants, and loafers without socks.

When Sennett showed up, Barnes demanded proof or evidence of who he was. As soon as Sennett showed his badge, Barmes seemed taken back. "What's this about?" he asked.

"Can we come in?" Sennett asked.

Barnes nodded, and we walked into the hallway. Sennett introduced me, and we moved down the hall. There was a polished banister and two or three oriental rugs over a slate floor. On a mahogany table underneath a mirror was a photo of two men, one of them was Barnes. I assumed the other one was Jake Edwards. The afternoon sun was shining between the oak trees on the front lawn and through the living room windows. The light dappled on the white couches. He motioned us to sit down, and we faced him across a glass coffee table with fresh flowers.

After he acknowledged that he was Russell Barnes, Sennett got to the question quickly and told him there has been a kidnaping and said it might be something in which Jake Edwards was involved."

After listening, Barnes appeared afraid as beads of sweat formed on his forehead. While appearing shocked, he stood up for his roommate. "Not Jake. He loves kids, and I can't imagine him ever getting involved in something like that."

"Did he ever mention Sandra Wells's name to you?"

"You mean the woman he was a sperm donor for?"

Sennett nodded his head. "What did he tell you?"

Barnes wrinkled his nose like there was a bad smell. "He said he was a donor and that he signed off any parental rights. I think he wished he could have had the baby. Why do you ask?"

"The embryo was implanted, and recently, a baby girl was delivered. The problem is that the child was kidnapped from the hospital. We're now on a search for her. Do you know where Edwards is?"

Barnes's posture suddenly stiffened. "I can't believe that Jake would do such a thing. I will say this. He called me a day ago and said he was going out of town for a while, just someplace up north."

"Any idea where he is?"

"I wish I did. He didn't tell me. It was strange." Barmes was gripping the sides of his head, like he didn't want to hear anything."

"How about other friends or family?"

"His father died when he was a child. His mother lives in Howell, Michigan. He told me they used to be very close, and then they had a falling out. I don't know much more than that."

I could see this was going to be a dead-end conversation. So did Sennett. He gave Barnes his card, and then we started walking back out of the house.

When he got to the door Barnes stopped him. "He called me before he left and said he was going up north."

Sennett did a double take. "What is going up north?"

"That's a common expression for going to upper Michigan. When I came home, the bedroom closet was open. He must have been looking for something like a duffle bag. His business clothes were there, but his backcountry clothes were gone."

"Anything else gone?" Sennett asked.

"It was a little strange. Jake liked camping, but he never told me where he was going."

"Any ideas?"

Barnes shook his head. "I don't know. Let me tell you, Jake and I are strictly friends and nothing else. He goes where he wants, and sometimes he is all over the map. When he came to Detroit, he became interested in his options. Most of the time he'd go to Northern Michigan or the Upper Peninsula. He likes camping on Isle Royal, surrounded by Lake Superior or going into Canada for canoeing in the Algonquin Park."

"I'm not saying he kidnapped anyone, but we have to chase down all the leads," Sennett said. "I guess we have our work cut out for us." He turned down the front hallway and reached for the front door.

Barnes hesitated for a moment. "Lieutenant, there is something else you should know. He took his gun."

"Did he usually take a firearm with him, especially if he was going to Canada?"

"Jake has dual citizenship and a permit to carry. He never had a problem going across the border."

Sennett tilted his head. "How long have you known Jake Edwards?"

"About six months." He stopped for a moment, as if something else came to his mind. It was almost an apology for living with Edwards.

We thanked Barnes and made our way back to my Wagoneer. As I opened the door, a piece of paper fell to the ground. I looked at it for a moment and it was attached to a metal clip. Before I could pick it up, Sennett grabbed my arm, pulled out a handkerchief from his pocket, picked the items up, and laid them out on the front seat. Then, he took out his cellphone and took photos of the papers. As he did, my eyes focused on the clip. It was strange.

"What's written on the paper?" he asked.

I gave it to him. He looked at it carefully on both sides. "I really can't make out the scribbling on the paper. Whoever wrote it had poor writing skills. It looks like *crisp* or something like that. Take a look at it." He handed it back to me.

I studied it carefully. When I gave it back to him, he put it in an envelope.

"Templeton told me that one of his agents talked with Edwards's mother," Sennett said. "She lives in Howell west of Detroit. Her husband died in a car accident a few years ago. She told him she wasn't close with her son and heard from him sporadically."

"Well, right now, Jake Edwards is our number one suspect." As I talked, I looked at my watch. I had promised Joey I would be home to spend some time with him.

CHAPTER 16

WHEN I CAME IN THE HOUSE, I saw Joey with his Lego project. There were pieces everywhere. I wasn't worried about the mess. He could almost put them together with his eyes closed. He looked up at me when I walked in, but he wasn't his usual ebullient self. He stared at me for a moment and then asked, "Dad, where is Baby Blue?"

Although I wasn't ready for the question, Jordan and I had decided not to tell him what was going on until we knew what had happened to our baby. Fortunately, he didn't give me time to answer.

"Mom, isn't feeling well," Joey said, "so Grandma came over."

The truth was that Jordan looked better. I think Joey wasn't used to her being home. She was tough, tougher than me. I could tell in her face that she was getting the fight in her back. I wasn't wrong. She listened as I told her about my conversation with Russell Barnes.

"Edwards must have been going somewhere in a hurry. You don't just walk out of your job as a public defender. People are depending on you. From what you told me, he doesn't sound like that kind of person."

"Even his friend thought it was strange. Something about him leaving with hiking boots on."

"Ben, I got a call from the lab guys," Jordan said. "I sent them the picture of the object you found on the ground. They came up with something interesting. They said it's an Othala rune."

"Huh?"

"It's something from an ancient alphabet. The Nazis adopted it as a symbol of white supremacists."

"I don't get it," I said.

"Neither do I. We need to find out more about Jake Edwards."

"Where do we start?"

"I think we need to speak with the people that know him."

"Since he and his mother don't speak to each other, I think maybe his professors would be helpful."

"Before you talk to them, I think you should look at what I found on Thomas Carlyle's blog," Jordan said.

"What about his blog? He is a right-to-life supporter."

"It's not that; it's the photo I saw." Jordan pulled up Carlyle's blog on her computer. After a couple of minutes, she came across a photo. It was a picture of Carlyle with another man, both with rifles in their hands. In between them was a six-point deer. In the back of the photo was a man that looked familiar, but I was never good on recognizing people.

"That's strange," I said. "The person in the back of the photo looks like someone in the photo I saw at Jake Edwards's home."

"Are you sure?" she asked.

I took out my cellphone and took a screenshot. When I was satisfied with the photo, I sent it to Sennett as a text.

A minute later, he was on the phone. "Where did you get that?"

I explained that Jordan found it on Thomas Carlyle's blog. "Do you think that guy in the back is Jake Edwards?"

"Not really. The guy I am really interested in is in the front of the photo. It's Jack Kilkearney. He was leading the march on the gun rights demonstration the day we ran into that melee at Grand Circus Park."

"What do we do now?" I asked.

"We have to leave that to Thomas Carlyle."

Chapter 17

It was strange returning to Carlyle's office for a second time in a week. Meeting him had seemed so straightforward when Jordan and I had first sat down in his office. Now the child of Sandra Wells's gift was kidnapped. So many emotions came with this place—great happiness and insurmountable despair. I had to hide my emotions into that spot in the back of my brain.

When we returned this time, I had the distinct feeling we were not wanted. It was a good thing Sennett was with me. A police order has a way of making people talk.

"We were looking at your blog and saw you and Jack Kilkearney together with a deer you killed," Sennett said. "Do you know him?"

Carlyle studied it for a moment. "That other guy in the photo is Tony Reynolds."

"I didn't know you knew him," Sennett said.

"It was a while ago. He is on the board of the Fight for Life Organization."

"What about Kilkearney? Are you a gun enthusiast?"

"Once in a while, I'll go with Kilkearney. Jack is also on the board." As Carlyle spoke, he fumbled with some papers on his desk. "Look ,Lieutenant, I've got a bunch of work to do. If there is something else you're looking for, I don't know what it is."

Sennett was cool. "The doc here and I just wanted to talk with you. A child has been kidnapped. We need to follow every lead." He smiled for a moment and said, "Just don't leave town."

Carlyle's face paled when he said it, but Sennett didn't respond. "Let's go, Ben."

As we walked out of Carlyle's office, we stopped by Alice Vandeveer's desk.

"Any word on that poor kidnapped child?" she asked.

"Nothing yet. If you ever have anything you want to tell us, here's my card." Sennett handed it to her, and we walked out of the office.

We took the elevator, and by the time we reached the ground floor, my ears needed to pop. I squeezed my nose on both nostrils and then tried to force air out. As I did, my ears popped open.

"What makes your ear pop when you get in an elevator?" Sennett asked.

"It's called your eustachian tube."

"Huh? Get to the lingo of us plebians," Sennett responded.

"It's the canal that runs from the back opening of your nose into the ear. The name is for the Italian anatomist who discovered it in the sixteenth century, Bartolomeo Eustachi. Evolution has created this anatomy to equalize pressure behind your ear drum. If your body didn't have it, a plane ride could really be painful."

"That and a few minutes on an elevator."

"You don't like going to the doctor, right?"

"I hate it. I'm always afraid they're going to find something," Sennett said.

"Relax, the worst that could happen is you'd have to see one, and he'll tell you how to do a Valsalva maneuver and take an over-the-counter nasal spray for a couple of days."

"Speak English. What the hell is a Valsalva maneuver?"

"Close your mouth, squeeze your nose on both sides, and try to blow your nose."

Sennett did it, and all of sudden, he smiled. "My ear is clear. You're a genius."

"Not me. Doctors think they have an answer for everything. It's what they don't know that I'm worried about." I smiled. "Medicine is like a ride on the elevator. We're human. Most of the time you succeed and sometimes you get the shaft."

"What do I do now?" Sennett asked.

"You're hopeless," I said. "Take two aspirins and call me in the morning, and if you see him, don't let him leave town."

"Huh? What's this don't leave town business?" Sennett asked.

"Scare tactics," I said. "Don't you know it always makes someone do something stupid? Right now, we must see Margaret Edwards."

Chapter 18

AFTER CALLING MARGARET EDWARDS, WE LEFT for Howell in the afternoon, driving on I-96 west through the farmlands and small towns of Southeast Michigan. Howell is northwest of Ann Arbor in Livingston County, one of the most politically conservative counties in Michigan. That would be no big deal, except for its history. For many decades, Howell had the reputation of being associated with the Ku Klux Klan. Most of this is due to a white supremacist leader and Michigan Grand Dragon named Robert E. Miles, who held KKK gatherings on his farm and at public auctions miles north of the city with a Howell address. Even after Miles died in 1992, they still had cross burnings.

After I told this to Sennett, he asked, "Is the KKK still there?"

"I think they've gone underground, but even up to 2000, they were selling KKK paraphernalia at public auctions on Martin Luther King's birthday. It didn't stop with white robes. The schools tried to suspend students for bearing a Confederate flag and taunting gay students with slurs. I think a lot of the bigotry and racism has been cleaned up, but you never know."

"With some people, it's never cleaned up," Sennett said. "It's tough to be a cop."

I nodded my head. "Yeah, bigots and racists never let it go. That's why haters are still fighting about who killed Ali in the sixteenth century. It's all about hate."

Sennett nodded his head. "I think you're right. It's the same for almost everyone. The Ku Klux Clan was originated by a Confederate general named Nathan Bedford Forest. For the South, he was a legendary cavalry general. The things he did after the Civil War were despicable.

"Selling hate is a terrible thing," I said. "Some people thrive on it. How does a police officer, deal with it?"

Sennett's face reddened. "We take an oath to serve and protect. For most policemen, they take it seriously. But it's not easy for everyone. Black, Jew, or Evangelist, we're always fighting for things that white people take for granted."

Our conversation was over as we reached the outskirts of Howell. That was the most I had ever heard Sennett talk about racism. Because of that, I figured that he didn't expect much when we drove up to Howell in the midday heat.

As a city, Howell seemed like every other small town that surrounded Detroit. In reality. it is just another sleepy, small town in the Midwest. There are small accessory stores, a Rite Aid, and even a winery. As we drove down Clinton Street, what wasn't there was an easy way to find street signs. I put the address on my cellphone. Even with the app, it took us a while to find Margaret Edwards's home outside of Howell on Lake Chemung.

"Man, you can find anything with that cell phone," Sennett said.

"Maybe a lot, but let's not carried away."

At two o'clock, we drove up to her house, a large two-story colonial hidden by thirty-foot oak trees along a paved driveway. We parked the Wagoneer next to a silver-grey Mercedes and walked up the flagstone walkway past neatly cared-for planted beds, lined with hostas and filled with daylilies and hydrangeas with large white snowball flowers. Sennett flicked the brass door knocker and waited.

After a couple of minutes, the door opened, and a blond-haired woman appeared in a tight, short-sleeved V-neck shirt, giving us a peek to both her cleavage and a hint of firm nipples on each side. Her tight, khaki-colored shorts enhanced her athletic body, and her face was smooth, making herself look younger than she probably was. With all that had happened, it made me feel guilty, but I couldn't help but notice. Her most interesting feature were her blue eyes. They immediately reminded me of my Baby Blue. Mrs. Edward looked at us both but spent more time on

Sennett. I didn't want to be judgmental, but she made it seem like this was the first time she had ever seen a Black man.

Sennett was unfazed as he pulled out his badge and started to ask questions. "As you know from our brief conversation, we want to ask you some questions about your son. The gentleman with me is Dr. Benjamin Dailey. Dr. Dailey's wife delivered a baby girl from a frozen embryo. The sperm donor was your son. We have not found the kidnapper. Are you aware that your son is a person of interest?"

"I saw an article in the newspaper and on the evening news," she said. "I don't care who is covering this, but my son has never been a troubled child, nor has he ever gotten into something like this in his life. I'm going to send out some kind of notice on social media and tell the world about my baby's kidnapping."

She seemed in control of herself and motioned us to come in and sit down in her living room. We sat down in large leather chairs, facing the lake. The furniture reminded me of the Restoration Hardware store that Jordan once showed me. The lake view stretched out in front of us through the large living room floor-to-ceiling window, I guessed, for about a half a mile. On the back of her lot, there was a hundred-foot dock built over swampy, shallow water to a small pontoon boat.

My gaze turned to the walls with artwork. They weren't made by amateurs. I studied art history in college and recognized one of them as a Roy Lichtenstein intaglio. I know they didn't come cheap. On a table below the painting was an artifact that looked like a series of multicolored balls wired together in a spiral twist.

"Interesting sculpture. It's almost like one of those atomic chemical diagrams I used to study in chemistry," I said.

Her face flushed for a moment. "It is. A friend of mine worked in a chemistry lab at the university. She gave it to me. She called it "The Carbon Atom at Work.""

My eyes shifted to an end table next to the couch. There were three photographs. On one end was a picture of Margaret Edwards in running gear at some type of running event, possibly a marathon. "Runner?"

"I ran the Chicago marathon a few times. That picture was taken last year."

I looked at the second picture with Margaret, a child and a handsome older man smiling at the photographer. "I assume the child is Jake.

Who's the other man?"

"You're right. That is Jake. The man on the left is his dad, Mike." She stopped, blinked her eyes for a moment, and then looked wistfully out the window toward the lake. "Mike died in an accident when Jake was fifteen years old."

Sennett looked at the third photo of a now grownup Jake Edwards in a graduation robe and a mortar board on his head. Next to him was a tall man dressed in a suit and smiling at him.

"That's a picture of Jake at his graduation from law school. The man is Anthony Reynolds from Grand Rapids. He was Mike's best friend. After Mike passed, Tony took over, and he and Jake did everything together. He took Jake hunting, fishing, and sailing. Mostly in Canada."

"Hard to imagine Jake was eighteen in that picture. Nice looking young man," I said.

"He is, except I wish the photographer would have taken it from the other side. See that damn bump on his left ear? Makes him look like an elf. Come to think of it, you're a doctor, aren't you?"

"Yeah, why?"

"Do you operate on those kinds of things?"

I nodded. "Yeah, I've done it. It's no big deal."

"Do you mind if we take photos with our cell phone of these photographs?" Sennett asked.

"I suppose there is no problem. You'd get them anyway."

Being a head and neck surgeon, I looked closer at the photo over Sennett's shoulder. It was a small-pointed nodule on the top of the ear. Frankly, I barely noticed it. I thought Jake's mother was being a little too critical. In the medical books, it's called Darwin's tubercle, a very common finding. In real life, it is just a hereditary bump that nature offers. As a doctor, I found out a long time ago that none of us are perfect.

Sennett nodded and took pictures with his cellphone and then asked, "Not to be too intrusive, but was Jake close with his dad?"

She hesitated for a moment, looked back at the photo, then cleared her throat, and spoke softly. "Mike never lived to see him graduate. Jake adored Mike. As I said, after Mike died, Tony Reynolds kind of took over and mentored him." As she spoke, her eyes watered.

"Sounds like things worked out."

"Well, that depends on whether you are the parent. Jake was a handful.

He was always in some kind of trouble. Fights on the playground, arguing with his teachers, that kind of problem. Not serious, but he never took the easy route to get what he wanted."

"Does your son still have contact with Mr. Reynolds?"

"Tony is the congressman from Grand Rapids. While Jake was in law school, I asked Tony to talk to him once in a while to focus him on getting his degree. I think that was why Jake became a lawyer."

"Are you and Mr. Reynolds still friends?" Sennett asked.

She blinked for a moment and then started talking. "We see each other once in a while. But I still haven't gotten over Mike's death. It would seem strange." She stopped talking, and her face turned serious. "I have to say the baby's kidnapping hit the news and made me very upset. After it happened, I sent out pacifiers to the public as a reminder to help find the baby. After all, it is the child of my son, frozen embryo or not."

When I asked her where Jake could be found, she ducked the question. Her face quickly paled.

"If you're looking at Jake as a criminal, you're barking up the wrong tree. First a sperm donor and then a kidnapping? No way. He respects the law. Do we know the recipient of the sperm donation?"

"Remember, we're not saying he did anything wrong," I said. "We're just investigating. The woman's name was Sandra Wells. She was a law student with your son at the university."

"You should know," Sennett interjected as he looked at me, "that Dr. Dailey is a member of the Detroit Police Department."

Her eyebrows knitted as she stared hard at me for a moment. I didn't know if the look was pity for my intrusion into her home or disgust for her son who had started the trouble.

"If you don't mind me asking, how did your husband die?" Sennett asked.

"It was several years ago. He had a heart attack. His car got out of control, and it went into the Rouge River outside of Ann Arbor." Her voice was steady as she spoke, but her posture was one of defiance.

"I'm sorry. I had to ask."

She turned her head, eyes widened, and then stared pensively at the lake. "It's okay. As I said, he died several years ago. I've come to grips with it. But this kidnapping of a baby is the one that I read about in the paper. That's awful. I didn't know Jake was the donor." She paused a moment and looked back at the photo. "I guess I'd be the grandmother. I love Jake. He's my only child. I always hoped he would have a child." She shuddered slightly when she said it.

Sennett must have noticed because he interjected. "I want to assure you that we're not here to discuss the legality of ownership, but we have been assured by the attorney who wrote the papers that Dr. Dailey and his wife are the legal parents." Sennett continued while touching his fingertips. "A child that is in the womb of its mother is not technically a person. But by legal fiction, an unborn child as an embryo is considered already born. He or she is granted a certain legal personality. If the child is born alive, it will then enjoy legal status." He went on to explain that Western law protects the individuals' rights of control and their interests in parenthood. Embryos are approached instrumentally, not by reference to any inherent characteristics that may be attributed to them outside the law. Politics may get into legal approaches, such as by prohibiting embryo preservation and limiting numbers, but they must be left to natural degeneration. In treating human embryos as property, courts recognize owners' power of how they want to keep the embryo."

"How do they determine ownership?" she asked.

"Ownership is not clear. If a couple gets divorced and they have frozen embryos, the embryos may be destroyed." Sennett added, "I assume Jake is gay. Am I right?"

"Why did you say that?" she asked.

"We assumed that because he lives with a guy."

Her eyes seemed to droop as he said it. "I don't think he is. That guy is a friend. Jake just doesn't care. It all started when his dad died." A teardrop made its way down her cheek. She reached for a tissue on the table next to her and dabbed her face. "I don't see my son often. I'm resigned to the fact that I will never have grandchildren. Jake is my only child. Regardless, I love him as only a mother can. I love him for who he is."

Sennett continued. "At present your son is the chief suspect in the kidnapping. But being a suspect is not a conviction. We intend to find him and determine what to do. When is the last time you saw or spoke to him?"

Her brow furrowed as she said that she spoke to him last week. Then she added that they were close, and couldn't believe that he would be involved in a kidnapping.

"Did he ever mention that he was the donor for Sandra Wells's embryo?"

"Jake was a very gregarious kid. After Mike Edward's father died, everything changed for him. He kind of went into a shell."

Sennett asked if money was a problem for Jake.

She said that Mike left a considerable amount of money to Margaret Edwards, plus a life insurance policy. "How else could I keep living in a fancy house?"

"Did he have a lot of friends?" Sennett asked.

She said that he always had friends, but just how close they were, she didn't know.

"If he had to go to a place, where would that be?"

"Probably the Algonquin Park in Canada. Mike had a lumber business in Canada. After I married him, we moved out to Toronto. That was where we spent much of our life. Jake loved it out there." She smiled as she said it. "I loved it there too, but after my husband died, I never went back."

"Do you still have the lumber business?"

She spoke in a warm caring voice. "The business is still there, but I could never bear to go back to Canada. I still get money from it, but I wanted to be on my own. Then through a friend, I got a job offer to work in Michigan for an executive office. I need to be busy."

Sennett nodded. "Do you know any of Jake's friends? People he was close to?"

"Jake always had friends. Growing up, he played a lot of sports and loved going camping. The only one I know now is Russell Barnes, his roommate. If anyone would know, it would be Russell."

"Did you ever meet Sandra Wells?"

"Sure. He brought Sandra to my house for dinner. Real nice person. I knew she was in law school with Jake. At one point I thought they were more than just friends. Then there was the murder. I read about it in the papers."

"How long have you lived here?" Sennett asked.

"I grew up in Howell. When Mike passed, I bought this place with the insurance money. It's a great house. C'mon, I'll show you the lake."

Sennett nodded, and we followed her out the back door. Walking down to the lake, we saw a pontoon boat there. As I followed behind Margaret, I tried not to look for the maker of her shorts. We stepped on the boat and sat down on a bench behind the steering well. Margaret started the engine and then took the rope off a cleat on the walkway. I went to the back and released the rear rope. When we were free from the dock, she put the throttle down, and we started down the lake.

She seemed at ease as the boat slid past handsome houses with manicured lawns. It was a pretty inland lake with small sailboats and a few ski boats with kids on slalom skis weaving in and out of their wakes. One of them seemed coming straight for us with the driver looking at the back of the boat. I don't think Margaret knew there was a problem. I was about to say something when the boat looked like it was headed for the pontoon. Now Margaret saw it too and yelled at them and waved her arms. They didn't notice. She tried to swerve the ponton, but its response was slow.

The ski boat was near us now. The kids inside were laughing. About fifteen feet from the pontoon, they swerved, sending a large wave against our boat. Suddenly, as the wave hit, the pontoon went upward. Margaret wasn't expecting it. She tried to maintain her balance, but her flip flops slid on the wet floor. She fell and then slid toward the opened door and onto the back of the ski boat. It didn't take long for her to get up. I think these kids were surprised at her agility because they moved to the front of the boat. The driver was trying to get away when she reached him and grabbed him by his shirt. She must have known judo because she spun him around and hit him in his abdomen with a foot kick. He fell breathless as she took a rope and bound his arms. Meanwhile, his buddies huddled at the back of the boat.

Then she jumped in the water. It was clear when she hit the water that she was not a swimmer. Sennett shut the throttle down. By this time Sennett had jumped up and took the wheel as I threw the life ring from the side of the pontoon to her. Panic filled her face as she grabbed it.

"Just hang onto the ring," I yelled. "I'll pull you in."

It seemed as if it took forever, but I managed to get her to the side ladder. She put her hands on it, and I bent over to pull her up. I got her to the edge and then to the floor. As she stood up, her wet body glistened from the bright sunshine. When she realized she was safe, she put her arms around me and squeezed her chest against mine. Then she looked up and smiled with something more than gratitude. "Thank you," she said. "I'm going to get the sheriff to get after those kids. You two just might get a call."

Ben extricated himself from her arms and turned to Sennett. "From the looks of it, you can take care of yourself," I said.

"I hope so. My mother had me take karate lessons when I was a kid. That's not all. Just in case, she took me to a gun range to show me how to take care of myself. She said a woman needs to know how to defend herself."

"You mother was right," I said. "But the best way to defend yourself is to avoid trouble."

She laughed.

"It's all yours now, George," I said.

"No problem. I already called."

We waited a few minutes, and, sure enough, there was the sheriff's boat heading toward us. Sennett pointed at the ski boat. By this time, the kids in the boat weren't laughing. When the sheriff's boat came near to the pontoon, I explained what had happened. He took it more seriously when Sennett showed his badge. Apparently, he knew the kids who played this prank and was going to go after them. It took five minutes for him to stop them in front of the pontoon.

The oldest boy seemed like the leader. He had that punk arrogant look as he slouched down on the seat in his runabout. His sullen appearance reflected his respect for the law. He knew what was coming.

"You boys aren't going to be so happy when your parents see the reckless driving ticket I'm giving you. If you don't pay it, we have ways to deal with you. For the next week you're off the lake. Got it?"

Their heads hung down. Hot days in the summer and losing their boat can do that to you. In this case they deserved it.

As the officer pulled up next to the pontoon and looked at Margaret Edwards, he stopped for a minute or two.

"You're Mrs. Edwards, aren't you?"

She nodded. "You've got to stop these kids. I could have been killed."

"We're on it," he replied, as he wrote her name in his notebook. "By the way, we got a notice of a kidnapping at City Hospital. Your name was mentioned as the mother of the man who is reported as a person of interest. Do we need to take sonny boy down to the headquarters?"

She gazed across the lake and nodded her head. Before she had a chance to speak, Sennett identified himself and me.

"Just give them a tour of the police station," she said. "They're the village ruffians. Please, let us go back to the house."

The sergeant reassured her that he would take care of the kids who had scared her.

Then, she started the pontoon, brought it back to her dock, and tied it to a cleat.

Sennett asked if she needed help, but she declined. It was close to six o'clock when we left. Once back in the Wagoneer, we sat for a few minutes trying to digest had just happened.

CHAPTER 19

Sennett and I pulled out of Margaret's driveway and drove to a gas station. While I filled the tank, he checked his cellphone and wrote something in his notebook during the call. Still on the phone, he squinted at what he wrote. I got back in the car and parked it on the street. After ten minutes he put the phone down.

"I spoke to Knudsen," Sennett said. "According to him, this guy Tony Reynolds must be the most famous man in Grand Rapids. He spent a tour in Vietnam as a Green Beret. When he came back, he went to law school at Boise State. Apparently, he was involved with a conservative political action group. There was a photo in a file I found that showed him holding an American flag and a placard that said Life Is for the Living, Stop Abortion. He worked in a law firm for a year and then moved to Grand Rapids. Once there, he joined another law firm known for its right-to-life organizations."

"If I could ask, what do you want to find out about this guy?"

"Evidence 101. Every suspect has information. They teach that at the academy. We have a right-to-life politico, a gun rights activist, and an attorney with a right-to-life blog. Sounds like a match made in heaven."

"Of all things, why did he move to Grand Rapids?" I asked. "Was it a woman?"

"When I spoke to Templeton, he said Reynolds had no trouble with the ladies, but he never married."

"Does he have a big influence on Jake Edwards?"

"As far as we know, Reynolds sees him now and then. Kind of like a Dutch uncle. Apparently, he talked Edwards into going to law school."

"I get the feeling that Mike Edwards's death had a big influence on everyone in the family, but in different ways. It was around that time that Jake Edwards went to college and then law school. He was on his own."

"Well, what do you think?" Sennett asked me.

"First of all, I couldn't believe how quick the cops came when you called them. She must have some clout with the locals. If that was my kid we were trying to find, I'd be all over it. Then there's this guy Reynolds in Grand Rapids. Now we have two places Jake might be going to, one in Grand Rapids and one in Canada. Pretty hard to get a search party. What do you think of Mrs. Edwards?"

"Aside from dealing with those kids, she was all over you. What's up with that?"

"I could care less. I have other issues to take care of."

Sennett looked sheepish. "Sorry, I didn't mean any disrespect. It's just her attitude. We've got a lot of country to cover. The only other people that can handle this is the FBI. We need to get hold of Templeton."

"There's one other thing," I said. "What about the issue that her son is gay?"

"I don't think his mother is judgmental," Sennett said. "Besides, because he stood up for gay rights in college and lives with a gay man, that doesn't mean he has changed his lifestyle. That's all his business. People have beliefs and issues. We can't be judged on personal likes and dislikes. Believe me, I know all about prejudice. If we do, we'll be causing more problems than we solve."

Suddenly I remembered where I had seen the other picture, the one of Tony Reynolds, in her living room. It was also at Thomas Carlyle's office. I started the car and then put a stick of Juicy Fruit in my mouth and immediately began grinding on the plastic-like chew. It took about a half-mile of driving until it was tasteless, just in time to get on the interstate. I put in another stick.

"You're going to grind your teeth to a nub, Doc."

"I'm betting the gum is going to outlast my teeth."

"Not strong enough with those jaws."

"You know gum is made from the sapodilla tree or synthetically with isobutylene. They also use it for inner tubes."

"Nice, remind me to keep riding my bike in case I get hungry."

"I am so frustrated," I said. "It seems as though there are only a few people left for us to get information. Edwards is one of them. You said most of these kidnappings are family induced. If he is, we have to find him. Where do we start?" I was not going to allow this to get away.

Sennett called Templeton and told him what happened. Nodding his head, he told me, "It's hard to go on a wild goose chase. Templeton said the FBI was sending out pictures of Jake Edwards and notifying the authorities around the country. You'd be surprised with how well that can work. Local knowledge can bring a lot of information."

We were on the outskirts of Detroit when Sennett's phone buzzed. It was Knudsen again. To say Sergeant Knudsen was reliable is an understatement. He was regular army in the service, and he transferred that dedication to his job on the force.

I glanced over at Sennett nodding his head. He told Knudsen to have Templeton call him. He clicked off and sat silently, looking out of the window as if he was thinking of what to say. He finally put his phone in his jacket and looked over at me. "They found one of those hospital tags in a motel in Ogalala, Nebraska. It had your daughter's name on it."

I almost swerved off the lane but then quickly straightened out the car and slowed down into the right lane. "Where was it?"

"It was at a Motel 6. Apparently, the cleaning lady brought it to the manager. He had received the FBI missing person notice and called the cops. The room was taken by a John Smith. He paid with cash."

"What do you make of it?"

"We need to speak with Templeton." Sennett pulled out his phone, put it on speakerphone, and dialed a number.

Templeton answered.

"What do you think about this?" Sennett asked.

"I checked out the name tag. It had City Hospital printed on it. I sent the photo to St. Vincent's, and they confirmed it was from their hospital."

"Were there any prints?" Sennett asked.

"That's where it gets dicey," Templeton said. "They have Jake Edwards's fingerprints on a Coke bottle. He has a fingerprint as part of his job with the city. It was a perfect match to the ones on her bracelet. They spoke with the manager of the motel and showed them a picture of Edwards. They thought it could have been him as the person in the motel, but facial recognition can be tricky."

"Where do you think the kidnapper is going?"

"Right now, it seems out west."

"That's a pretty big area," Sennett said.

"The FBI is going to focus on the Hamilton, Montana, area because the family was associated with a home in Idaho."

Sennett then told Templeton about their visit to Edwards's mother. Templeton said they were already on their way to see her.

It was hard to drive and listen to Sennett. My instant reaction was to go to the airport, get on a plane, and head for Idaho. My common sense told me to stay with Jordan. She needed my help, and going on a wild goose chase wouldn't accomplish much. I told Sennett I'd be staying here.

He seemed relieved. "I thought you might think about going rogue. We're going to find Baby Blue, Ben. Trust me; we're going to find her."

Sennett never called me by my name unless it was important; it was always "Doc." I knew he meant what he just said. On the way back, I called Jordan and explained what had happened. The fact that the hospital bracelet was found seemed to energize her.

When we arrived at my home, Jordan was at her desk. Her computer was on, and she stared at the screen, almost not seeing us. When she looked up, I could almost feel the intensity in her eyes that she usually reserved for a case she was trying. "I'm interested in Thomas Carlyle," she said calmly. "We need to find out what Mr. Carlyle has to say." She had the computer set up and Carlyle's blog on the screen.

Sennett sat behind her desk, and I pulled up a chair next to him.

After an hour, we had gone through three-quarters of the blogs. Sennett looked like he was tiring and ready to quit when he came to a page and stopped. On the screen were three men in hunting gear holding rifles. They were kneeling on the ground next to a six-point buck they had probably shot. I read the blog with Sennett. It was designed to show how this young man who had become a well-known outdoorsman almost had been aborted as a fetus. That wasn't the reason Sennett read the blog. "See that guy with Carlyle?"

I nodded. "Looks like your average deer hunter."

"He's more than average."

"Why?"

"His name is Jack Kilkearney. Does that ring a bell?"

"Yeah," I said. "He's that gun rights guy from the demonstration at Grand Circus Park. Right?"

Sennett nodded. "That's right."

"What does that have to do with my daughter's kidnapping?" I said, choking out the words.

"Gun powder on the nursery room floor, a relationship between your adoption lawyer and Kilkearney, the leader of the gun rights demonstration. I don't believe in coincidence."

"Okay, so what does that prove?"

"I don't know. Sometimes these photos are publicity shots. Our first job is to see if Kilkearney knew Carlyle."

"Who is the other guy?" I asked.

"We need to make another visit with Alice Vandeveer."

A T THREE IN THE AFTERNOON, WE called Carlyle's office, and fortunately, he wasn't there. Alice Vanderveer was. We wanted to meet with her outside of the office. She said Carlyle had left for the day. Sennett suggested we go down to Savannah Blue, a restaurant a couple of blocks from the building to talk. When we arrived, Alice was already there. We sat down and studied the menu. When the waiter came up, Sennett ordered the catfish fritter, and I took the jumbo crab cakes. Alice ordered a kale caesar salad.

"You must know by now that there has been a kidnapping of Dr. Dailey's newborn daughter," Sennett started.

"I read about it in the paper. I can't tell you how upset I am for you, Dr. Dailey, and your family. That's why I came to meet with you." Thankfully, she had kind words and a soothing tone.

Sennett nodded and then went on to explain that, in our search for clues, the department went on to Mr. Carlyle's blog and showed her a photo of Jack Kilkearney with him. When she asked why the photo was important, he told her that they found traces of gun powder on the floor of the nursery that might be associated with the recent gun rights march.

It took her a moment. "Now that you mention it, I remember him. His name is Jack something."

"Kilkearney?" Sennett replied.

"That's it. He and Mr. Carlyle go deer hunting every year."

"Is there anything specific you can remember about him?"

"I know he is very religious and supports right to life. He and Mr. Carlyle go out to Northern Michigan every year for some kind of convention or meeting. Then they go hunting in North Dakota. Mr. Carlyle showed me this photo of a an eight-point buck he shot with some friends. I don't know how the photo got in Jake Edwards's file."

She passed the photo to me. There were five people in it. "Do you know these people?" I asked.

"Well, this young man is Jake Edwards, probably in his early twenties."

When I looked, the most I got from it was a side headshot. But after looking at it, I could feel there was something odd about the photo. I was irritated because I couldn't place it. Next to him was a man in a camouflage shirt and a rifle at his side.

Before she had a chance to tell me who it was, Sennett pointed him out. "Looks like Jake Edwards hangs out with a tough crowd," he said. "Jack Kilkearney was behind the demonstration at Grand Circus Park."

"Who are the other three?" I asked.

Alice picked up the photo. "The one on the left is Mr. Carlyle. Next to him is Anthony Reynolds. He's the congressman from Grand Rapids. I've never met him. When I made reservations for them, Mr. Carlyle said he was a friend of Mr. Reynolds's."

I stared at the photo. The man in question was wearing a hunting jacket. His face was partially covered by a Stetson Cruiser and a thick beard, heavy eyebrows, and deep-set, dark eyes.

"Mr. Carlyle told me you have to have a certificate to hunt in the Dakotas," Alice said. "He didn't tell me how much it cost, but I heard him talking with the other man and telling him he'd better get his money's worth."

"Do you remember where the hunting took place?" Sennett asked.

"Some state recreational area or something like that."

"North?" I asked.

She snapped her fingers. "Maybe it was North Dakota."

"Do you have any records of where exactly it was?"

"I sure do. I make the arrangements. I even get the e-bikes for the hunting."

By now, we had finished eating. Alice suggested we return to the office so she could access some information on her computer, so we paid and walked back to her building. In the office, she went on to her computer and pulled up a screen. Once she found it, she wrote something down and handed it to me.

I looked at the paper. It said *The Right to Life March*.

"Do you have any idea where they stayed in North Dakota?" Sennett asked.

She looked again and then wrote the name on another piece of paper: J. Clark Salyer Nature Wildlife Refuge..

"Who is the other man in the photo?" Sennett asked.

"His name is Earl Crandall, but I assumed he worked with Mr. Reynolds. I think he worked at City Hospital."

"What do you know about him?"

"All I know is he was always asking me to do things. I already have a boss. I must have had ten calls from him telling me that Mr. Reynolds wanted this and that. It was irritating. He works at City Hospital and Mr. Reynolds knows him."

I took my cellphone out and clicked a picture of the photo.

"What did Mr. Reynolds do? Was he in politics?" Sennett asked.

"I was told that he is a five-term congressman from Western Michigan, you know, Grand Rapids, Holland, that area. He ran as a conservative, gun rights, right-to-life politician, even noted to have spoken to some white supremist groups. As far as I know, he acted like he owned half the state," she replied. "Anyway, that's what someone told me."

"Do you know the name of his business?" I asked.

"It was a funny name, something like Backcountry Lumber."

"When Mr. Carlyle returned, I asked him how his trip was. He said they got a trophy six-point buck. I don't know much about hunting." She paused for a moment. "There's one other thing. I do remember that Mr. Reynolds was planning to retire from Congress and move out of Grand Rapids. I had to track him down and found that his current home is in Northern Michigan."

"Any idea where?"

She looked through the contacts and found the location in Northport.

I asked her if I could take a snapshot of the picture with my cellphone.

She nodded and shared the address with me. I then emailed it to Sennett.

We thanked her and made our way back to the car. When Sennett sat down and locked the door, he picked up his phone and called Knudsen. He wanted to know everything about Reynolds and Jake Edwards's father.

After he finished, I told Sennett, "There's something strange about Tony Reynolds. He's a well-known congressman. How would he fit in this kidnapping? Can you place it?"

"Knudsen's checking him out.

It took Knudsen more time than usual, but after an hour, he sent Sennett all the information he could find. Sennett looked it over for fifteen minutes and then put down his phone and put some more notes in his book. "Anthony Reynolds must be one of the most famous men in Grand Rapids. I checked out a guy in Idaho named Fenchly. According to Knudsen, apparently, at one time, Reynolds had the largest logging business in the Northwest. He spent a tour in Vietnam as a Green Beret. He was educated at Boise State and started his logging business in Idaho. Now, he seems to be known more for his philanthropy and his politics. There were several articles on him."

"Why do we want to investigate this guy?"

"Evidence 101. Every suspect has information. They teach that at the academy. We have a right-to-life politico, a gun rights activist, and an attorney with a right-to-life blog. Sounds like a match made in heaven."

"What are you going to do now?"

"It's out of my jurisdiction. Templeton called him. He said he has yet to speak to Jake Edwards."

"What about Jake's father?"

It's everything they said. He was driving in a snowstorm. His car rolled into a river running next to the highway. According to the coroner the cause of death was drowning. An autopsy showed he had a coronary artery blockage."

I sat for a moment, perplexed with all this knowledge of my child's father. Why couldn't this be just a great birth and a happy ending? "Boy, it makes you wonder what makes people believe in God."

"I'll agree with that," Sennett said.

"I took a course in college on philosophy. The professor was big on natural law. I was at that stage when I questioned religion and asked him in class how people can claim there is a God when you can't see or touch or speak to him or her."

"What did he say?"

"He quoted St. Thomas Acquinas who said it's the difference between conceiving and perceiving."

"Huh?"

"Conceiving is when you can build something, like making a square that you can see and touch. Perceiving is seeing the square in your mind without actually building it."

"Would good and evil fall into that?" Sennett asked.

"I guess that it depends on the good and evil. But I will say this, perceiving something you can't see is hard, but it can make you reach out to the unknown."

"For what has happened, I hope your perception is good."

SENNETT CALLED TEMPLETON AT THE FBI and put the call on speakerphone so I could listen in. Sennett stalked the room like a caged animal. It was clear everyone was stuck in the same void. When he finished, Sennett slowly put his notepad back in his pocket. "Nothing to report. Edwards lived with his parents until he was fifteen. His father died in the accident. Apparently, his father was a very successful businessman in lumber."

"Why did Jake Edwards and his mother leave?"

"Good question. Reynolds had a large estate in Idaho near the entrance to the Selway- Bitterroot Wilderness. The FBI sent a crew up to the house to search it. Templeton talked to Reynolds. He said he took Jake and his mother there for a couple of weeks after Jake's father died. The Idaho State Police checked out the house. It's still there. They said it was empty, but it is continuously maintained. According to them, the place was rented out by companies for corporate outings. Regardless, he said there was no evidence that Edwards or the child was there."

"Anything else?"

"The police took photos of everything in the house. He's sending them to me as an attachment in an email. I'll send it to you."

We waited for a few minutes, and the images appeared. The detailed photos showed a substantial wooden structure, a log cabin on steroids. Pictures of the inside showed large rooms, bedrooms, and what appeared to be a dining room and a library.

As we looked at them, I suddenly said, "Stop! Go back to the start of this room."

"What are you looking at?'
"Look at the door. What do you see?"
"A door?"
"What about the carving on the door?"
Sennett looked again. "It looks like some kind of a crazy paperclip."
"Exactly. I'll take a photo."

I reached in my pocket, pulled out the phone, and took a photo. "We need to find out what this means. If I send it to Knudsen, do you think he could find out?"

"There's nothing that man can't find out," Sennett said. "I'll give you his cell number. Send it, and I'll tell him what it's about."

I sent it and waited as Sennett told Knudsen what he wanted. In the meantime, we went down to the local coffee place and chugged down a medium regular. Just as we finished, Sennett's phone rang. I watched as he listened. I could see his eyebrows knitting and the corner of his mouth twitch.

"That Knudsen is the crime dog. He never quits. He said that the only thing they could match it to is a rune."

"Huh?"

"Catch this. A rune is a German letter. A white supremist uses it as a symbol of being a neo-Nazi."

"So this upright man is part of the neo-Nazi clan?" I asked.

"It's a story. We don't know if it's nonfiction. Apparently, the people of western Michigan love Reynolds. He's given out millions to conservative issues in the state. Always within the law."

"Has anyone spoken to Reynolds?"

"His administrator said he was in the Northwest, hunting. No one has seen him in the last two weeks."

"What's next?" I asked.

"There's something missing here," Sennett said. "Jake Edwards met Sandra Wells in law school. They became friends. When she worked to clear criminal investigation of the city hospital construction, she knew she was in danger and wanted a legacy. That's when she asked Jake Edwards to be a sperm donor for her. What happened next was certainly strange. She went to see you for a medical issue. According to Carlyle, she told him it was for an interview, in which she would decide whether you and Jordan would qualify to inherit the embryo in case anything happened to her. Carlyle wrote up the document, and you two accepted. All we know now is that Sandra Wells was murdered. We need to visit the people that knew Jake. I'd say going to his law school mentor would be a good place to start."

Chapter 21

After making a few calls, we found that Jonathon Edwards's faculty law advisor was Marlene Schultz. We made an appointment with her to see if there was something we had missed. Her office was in the law quad on the campus in Ann Arbor. We parked the car and made our way to her building. Schultz was on the second floor. We took the stairs.

Her office was a small room, overlooking the campus. I knocked on the door, and we were asked from inside to come in. When we entered, we faced a small woman with gray hair, brushed back in a ponytail. At first glance, she looked somewhat meek behind her desk, but once she started talking, she was all business.

The first thing she said about Jake Edwards was he had a chip on his shoulder. She took a pencil and tapped it against a notepad. As she spoke, she took out a book from behind her desk. "The professors got tired of his anger to the status quo. He was smart enough to realize that the law is not for everyone. That viewpoint started a lot of arguments. Most of the time, he won. It was relief for the faculty when he graduated."

"What kind of arguments?" Sennett asked.

"You know, if you said it was nice outside, he would say it's raining. Never satisfied."

"Did any of his anger turn into physical confrontation?"

"I think he found his niche working for the city as a lawyer. As you know, he went to the University of Michigan undergrad."

I asked Shultz his bona fides.

She looked at his record and found he graduated summa cum laude, law review, Order of the Coif, and the Lambda Society.

"Not bad for a troublemaker," I said.

She gave me a grimace and a slight shake of the head. "You're right. It's just that he had a personality that was engaging. I think he would have gone into politics."

"Why didn't he?

"People thought he was gay. I think he didn't want to make a public issue of his personal choices."

"What about Sandra Wells?"

"They were inseparable. Not physically, of course. They were just good friends."

"Did Mr. Edwards ever talk to you about his life? Friends, family issues, and goals for his future."

"I found out his father died in an automobile accident when he was in college. His mother raised him. I'll never forget his anger over his father's death. That was when Jake changed. He had a hard time accepting his father's death." She paused for a moment as if she remembered something.

"Did he ever come out of it?" I asked.

"Come to think of it, after the first semester was over, he did say he was going to Idaho to visit someone who was a friend of the family, a politician or something like that."

"Did he give you the name of this man?"

"It was an odd name. Kind of British. I remember all of this because one day he came to my office and told me he wasn't going back to Idaho. I asked him about it. That's when he told me he supported the gay movement. Apparently, the family friend found out about it and was told he wasn't welcome."

"That's a pretty stiff response. Was there anything else?"

"Not that I know of. This friend is a congressman from Grand Rapids, and you know how those kind of things muddy the political water."

I paused for a moment. "What about Sandra Wells?" I asked.

"He and Sandra were close friends. He told me about Sandra asking him to be a sperm donor. He wanted my opinion. I told him if he felt comfortable, he should do it. I got the feeling that she was in some kind of danger and wanted a legacy."

"She was right," I said. "She has her legacy. I'm sure you know the story." I went on to tell her about the kidnapping."

"I read about it. It certainly is a tragedy."

Sennett went on to explain the reason we were here. He mentioned that Jake was considered to be the main suspect in the kidnapping. Shultz responded that in no way would Jake Edwards do something like that.

"What about Jake's mother?" Sennett asked.

"I don't know much about his family. I guess you would have to speak with her."

"We've met."

We thanked Shultz and left to go back to Detroit. It was getting dark, and a mild drizzle covered the road when we picked up the car on State Street. I gave Sennett the keys, and we made our way back to the I-94 expressway. The evening rush was starting, but most of the drivers ignored the seventy-mile-an-hour limit. Sennett negotiated the car past several drivers moving in and out of the passing lane. Near the Southfield exit, a car moved to the left of us in the passing lane. As the car passed, I noticed the rear window lowered. What I saw next sent a chill down my spine. A gun popped through the window. I yelled, "Look out, George!"

Sennett swerved to the left, and the Jeep started to slide on the pavement. I felt helpless as the rear end slid past the shoulder toward the upcoming bridge abutment. Sennett countered the slide by decelerating and pointing his wheels in the direction he wanted to go. There was no panic. Slowly, the car began to regain the highway.

"Are you okay?" I asked.

Sennett nodded, but I could tell he was shaken up. No one stays calm in a near-death encounter.

"I'm glad you took the driving course."

"Am I thinking what you are?" he asked. "That was no accident."

"Yeah. Too late to find out. I didn't catch the license."

"Don't worry. We're lucky. Whoever it was, the individual was no amateur. Strange it would happen after our conversation with Reynolds."

"Neither were you," I said. "I'll remember this the next time we go for a ride."

When we made it back, I examined the damage. The rear bumper was bent and had a deep dent in it. Otherwise, it was drivable.

"I bet who'll get hell for this," I said.

"As long as it can be driven, they'll fix it and let it go."

It was after six o'clock when we arrived at police headquarters. He exited, and I drove home. When I walked in the house, Jordan was still in her pajamas. Ask any psychiatrist, and he'll tell you depression will do that to you. I told her about our meeting at the law school. I didn't mention the car ride back. She had enough on her mind.

CHAPTER 22

The following morning, I called Sennett. He seemed happier than I would have expected following the previous day's ride. "Any luck on finding out who tried to hit us?"

"It turns out there was a car behind. Someone saw the whole thing and phoned in to the police. He was even nice enough to get the license plate.

"And?"

"A stolen vehicle. So much for the good Samaritan."

"Anything else?" I asked.

"There was no information on Baby Blue. The FBI tried to trace her from the motel in Ogalala, but the trail went dry."

From my perspective, the fact Reynolds once lived in Idaho brought some interest as to the baby's disappearance in the West.

I was curious about Reynolds when I spoke to Sennett about him that afternoon. He said Knudsen found that the congressman's house in Grand Rapids was sold, and he moved to his home in Northport, a small town in Northern Michigan on the shores of Lake Michigan. I checked with his office, and they confirmed he was going to be in Northport.

"Why would this guy move to Northern Michigan after being in politics, making a fortune in Idaho, and being surrounded by a constituency of like-minded people?" I asked.

"Good question, Ben. Maybe it's a summer home. I think the answer needs to come from someone who knows him."

"Funny you should mention that," I said. "I got to talking with a patient a few weeks ago about fly fishing. It turned out he has a brother in Idaho who writes for a Boise newspaper. I asked him if he knew Reynolds. He said no, but he gave me the name of Rick Fenchly. I talked to him yesterday. He's the editor of the *Boise Idaho Register*. It didn't take long before we were on the phone. Fenchly seemed anxious to talk about Reynolds. The first thing he asked me was why did I want to talk about Dutch. I told him Jake Edwards may be involved in a kidnapping and he had contact with Reynolds some years ago. We had to touch all the stones. Fenchly said he knew Jake, was a nice kid. His father owned a lumber yard in Canada. He knew about the auto accident. Fenchly said Reynolds knew the family and tried to help.

"I asked why Reynolds was quitting the political life. Fenchly said Dutch Reynolds was a moonshot in Idaho. He had everything going for him, rich beyond contemplation from his lumber business. Then he moved to Grand Rapids, invested in some new lumber companies and after a couple of years ran for Congress. He had a lot of ideas that Michiganders liked. He put himself out there as an evangelistic Christian—second amendment rights, anti-abortion, and maybe even a trace of racism. Fenchly said the word was out that he might be run for the Senate in DC. He got texts every day about it, asking for money, thought Reynolds might even be aiming for the presidency.

"I asked how Jake fit in with Reynolds, and Fenchly said Reynolds probably wanted to stay away from the gay issues.

"It sounded as if Fenchly and Reynolds were not the best of friends. He said he initially liked the guy—knew him for twenty years, is smart, and genuinely cares for the rights of the people of state, that he'd fought for the environment, low crime, and a stable tax basis. But something changed. Fenchly said it was subtle, but about five years ago he seemed to be withdrawn, uninterested."

I told Sennett I asked about Reynolds's family. "Fenchly said the man has no kids, and his wife died in a home fire; there was a faulty electric circuit. He was never the same after that.

"I asked why Reynolds moved to Northern Michigan, and Fenchly thought he wanted a place to just get away from politics. And he chose

Northern Michigan because, as he told friends, he wanted to spend time in a different venue where he wasn't a politician. He loves to be on the water with his sailboat on Lake Michigan. Fenchly said Reynolds once mentioned Northport."

"We need to talk with Mr. Reynolds," Sennett said. "Do you think he might be willing to talk with us?"

"Good luck," I said. "You will definitely know more if he will talk to you. I'll make a call to Fenchly for contact info."

Twenty minutes later, Fenchly called me back. "I spoke to Adrian, his chief of staff. She said Reynolds left for his home in Northern Michigan and couldn't tell where he was right now. Adrian said she had direct orders not to call him unless it was an emergency."

"How do the people see it? Does he have a chance?" I asked.

"The people love him. He is very rich and knows how to use money. Through his donations, he has single handedly given millions of dollars to the hospitals in Grand Rapids. This money has put students through medical schools and created cutting-edge medical programs at the hospital and in the laboratory."

"I'd like to meet him," I said.

"Don't hold your breath. He is a man in motion."

"Do you really think he is a possible presidential candidate?"

"I don't know," Fenchly said. "Just remember, he doesn't quit. When he wants something, he usually gets it."

CHAPTER 23

I LEFT AND CALLED JORDAN TO TELL her what I had found out. As we talked, I could tell my trip was exasperating her. She needed me at home. I told her I couldn't sit still and not do something positive to find our child. We must have had the same parents because she couldn't sit still either. I reminded her that she reaches me frequently and constantly looks where I'm located because she had the phone locating device.

Most of her time was on the internet, looking for clues and talking to the Feds in her department. Regardless, there was still danger. She said she was thankful that after the kidnapping the police car across the street provided protection. Her being with Joey and the presence of a police surveillance on the street gave me some comfort too. But I remembered from past cases that it could help me just so much.

Besides, I had Sennett with me, and I was thankful for his presence. He called his girlfriend, Alicia, and asked if she would go over to my house. Jordan had met her before, and they seemed to take a liking to each other. I checked with Jordan, and she seemed happy to have the company, so Alicia stayed with her.

I knew how lonely life could be without someone you love. He knew Alicia was perfect for him. The conversation drifted to the kidnapping.

"Alicia told me someone came into her store before your daughter was born," he said. "Nice looking guy. Said he was a lawyer. He said he knew me and wondered if the couple had had their baby. I told him she didn't know."

Something was bothering me about the photo of Jake Edwards from the law school. I pulled it out and looked at it again. There was something odd about the appearance of Jake Edwards. I just didn't know what.

Sennett and I sat in his SUV, trying to figure out where to turn.

"This kidnapping was well-thought-out," Sennett said. "We have three people who might be involved or have information we need—Jake Edwards, Tony Reynolds, and Earl Crandall. Jake Edwards, for all intents, is probably not a suspect, and Tony Reynolds, who is in Northport, has reason to be involved. Unfortunately, Earl Crandall was the doctor from City Hospital. But you know what happened to him. I need Knudsen."

Knudsen called Sennett and told him to put him on speaker phone. "Lieutenant Sennett, I just got this call from an anonymous person. It turns out it was from Earl Crandall. All he said was "He Jiankui – Nature magazine." He even spelled it out and hung up. The call was from City Hospital."

"Spell that out for me."

He did.

Sennett wrote it out. "Any idea what it means?"

Knudsen had checked the internet, but he sounded frustrated. All he could find was an article in *Nature* magazine about a Chinese citizen who used a method called CRISPR to protect his family against HIV. He got in trouble with the Chinese government."

Sennett looked perplexed.

"How did this CRISPR get into the discussion?" Sennett asked me.

"George, trust me, they're going to make a doctor out of you. It has something to do about detecting and destroying DNA. You've got to read it. It was really scary. Our best chance to find out is to stay close to Alan Davis, the county coroner. He's a good source." I tried to call him, but he wasn't in.

In spite of it, I called Jordan and told her what was going on. She said she would look it up and call me.

She didn't take long. When I got home, she gave me a tutorial, trying to get me up to speed on CRISPR. That's not unusual. When Jordan is on the hunt for something, she is all in. She discussed an article she read about CRISPR. It claimed that CRISPR may be the next best thing in medicine. If the investigators could inject an enzyme called Cas9 into a patient, they could actually create new DNA. The reward for this is being able to cure diseases, such as cancer, by altering the DNA of the malignant cells. No wonder Jennifer Doudna got the Nobel prize in chemistry for her work on CRISPR editing.

What I couldn't come to grips with was what it had to do with Baby Blue. Then Jordan showed me a letter Jenniffer Doudna wrote after receiving the Nobel Prize. It included a short statement:

> *I had a dream recently, and in my dream—she mentioned the name of a leading scientific researcher—had come to see me and said, "I have somebody very powerful with me who I want you to meet, and I want you to explain to him how this technology functions." So I said, Sure, who is it? It was Adolf Hitler. I was really horrified, but I went into a room and there was Hitler. He had a pig face, and I could only see him from behind and he was taking notes and he said, "I want to understand the uses and implications of this amazing technology." I woke up in a cold sweat. And that dream has haunted me from that day. Because suppose somebody like Hitler had access to this—we can only imagine the kind of horrible uses he could put it to.*

Chapter 24

By the time I finished reading the letter and trying to figure it out, I was overwhelmed and groggy and went to bed. The next morning at six, the alarm woke me up. I got up early so I could meet Alan Davis, the coroner, at his office.

Davis and I went through medical school together. He graduated as the smartest student in our medical class. I didn't want to compete with his GPA. Let's just say, in my class, I graduated. The problem with him is that he made sure everyone knew where they stood relative to him.

When I got to the morgue, I found Davis fast asleep in his chair and snoring. I coughed and cleared my throat until he woke up with a start. When he heard me, I could see a twitch of disappointment on his face. For those four years in medical school, he hung around with the top guys in our class, except for me. He had little in common with an ex-football slug like me.

"What are you doing down here, Ben?" he asked as he rubbed his eyes. "Another case?"

He had been part of my near death as a physician, so "another case" was a big thing to him. "No, Al, this is something much bigger. It has to do with a kidnapping. The victim is my kid."

He sat up straight in his chair, took off his glasses, reached for a tissue, and started cleaning the lens. "Is this about the kidnapping at the hospital?"

I nodded.

"What does CRISPR have to do with it?"

I told him about the piece of paper that we found, including the drawing of a circle cut in half.

His initial response was he wouldn't know what to make out of the findings. "It's some kind of symbol. I haven't seen it before. There is one other thing. It's a big stretch to try changing the genetic makeup of an individual."

"Is it possible?"

"It is, but let me ask you a question, Ben. Do you look for trouble, or does trouble look for you?"

"It's a mixed bag."

"Well, since it's your family, I'll help. Tell me what the problem is."

"I told him about the kidnapping at the hospital and then the article in *Nature* that focused on CRISPR. I said it was strange to me, and what I had found so far was reiterating Doudna's dream.

"I saw that. It's science fiction, and I can't imagine it happening. But nobody knows yet."

"I understand, Al. What I need to know is whether it's possible."

Davis slithered his lanky frame out of his desk chair and looked out of his window to the morgue. While he fumbled with his pen, he didn't say anything and just stood there for a few minutes. I was going to ask him if he was okay, but he turned back to me and put his glasses back in his jacket. "I just remembered there's was a guy at City Hospital at its Institute for Biological Inventions named Earl Crandall. He was the person responsible for their frozen embryo project and was deeply involved in the DNA program. Unfortunately, because of a system failure of frozen embryos, there was a death of a couple of embryos."

"I know about Earl Crandall. He may have been somehow connected to the kidnapping of my baby and took the heat of the kidnapping and was terminated."

"What did he do?" Davis asked.

"He was on duty when the kidnapping occurred."

"In spite of that, it is protocol to get a DNA swab from the newborn child," Davis said.

"Where is Crandall working now?" I asked.

"Interesting you ask," Davis said. "I heard he moved to work at a

DNA lab in western Michigan. Outside of Berkley, California, most of DNA research is being done in specialty labs. There are several of these kinds of labs around the country. The nearest one here is in Kalamazoo. It's called Visionary Chemical Laboratory. You might try that."

"What do we know about Visionary Chemical?"

"It's part of the new wave for treating illnesses, specifically cancer. If you can change the DNA of the cancer cell, you can destroy its effect. It's a tremendous step forward."

Davis acted surprised at my interest in CRISPR.

"No one has ever done something like that I know of." Davis looked at me for a moment with a puzzled look. "Like I said, if this is a baby that you're looking for, they always do DNA swabs on the inside of the child's cheek. Do you know what they showed for your baby?"

I stumbled for an answer. "I don't know."

"What do you mean?" Davis asked.

"Apparently, they're looking for it."

Davis looked perplexed. "Somebody had to steal it. It's hospital rules to get DNA samples from a newborn."

"Somebody must not want us to know her DNA. We need to find Earl Crandall. I'll call Sgt. Knudsen," I said. "He can find anything."

CHAPTER 25

KNUDSEN SPENT THE BETTER PART OF a day to working on Crandall's history. According to his contacts, Earl Crandall wanted to be a doctor, but both his grades and his money were insufficient. His only choice for getting into a medical school was the Caribbean. A funding from a program in the States paid for part of his tuition. The balance was supported by a group in Grand Rapids. While he had average grades in his classes, he excelled in obstetrics and gynecology. He had even published an article on infertility and genetics. Because of it, he was able to transfer his credits to the United States. According to Knudsen, despite Crandall being a good student, the people he spoke to said he always had a chip on his shoulder over his rejection by American medical schools. He was told that while the Caribbean school offered a medical degree, it did not guarantee graduates acceptance and success at an American hospital. But Crandall was noted to be an excellent student.

When he graduated, he applied for an obstetrics and gynecology residency at City Hospital. The head of the department said there was an opening for him in their fertility program, mainly with frozen embryos. His position was to ensure the embryos were selected properly and, once in the freezing process, to make sure all the equipment was functioning properly. It was also his job to make sure the infants were tested properly. From what Knudsen was told, Crandall had developed a good reputation for running embryo programs, both from an administrative position and hands-on engineering. The administrator who originated the position gave him high marks in managing the care for the embryos. While it wasn't a medical license, Crandall was told that if he finished the residency and passed the state examination, he might get an appointment in the obstetrics department.

Knudsen said that Crandall did finish the obstetrics/gynecology residency and passed the state examination. His specialty was DNA evaluations of newborns. In addition to being the go-to guy for embryotic fertility management at the medical center, he was the coordinator for all DNA and laboratory tests. That was until the day the electrical incubators crashed. Some embryos were lost; it was a malfunction that could have been prevented. It turned out there was a defect in the electrical installation. They asked Crandall for an explanation. He didn't have any. Unfortunately, he took the fall. Already angry and irritating to be around, he claimed he would get even with the sons of bitches who caused the malfunction.

I guessed the hospital couldn't take on this second event. Crandall was responsible, although in the end, there was no evidence that Crandall was involved. But according to Knudsen, you know what rolls down hill, and Crandall was at the bottom. He was responsible for the absent DNA test.

Knudsen said Crandall stayed until his name was cleared. In the meantime, he found a job in Kalamazoo with a biologic company called Visionary Chemical.

I guessed his stay at City Hospital wasn't an amicable relationship from the way his boss described him. His past seemed to be his worst enemy. People referred to him again as a knowledgeable employee with a chip on his shoulder. He was still smarting from his leaving City Hospital.

Immediately, I asked Knudsen to get the DNA results for me of my daughter. It took five minutes for him to give me an answer. The problem was there were no results.

"The baby's DNA has to come from the parents," Knudsen said. "The problem is that some of the DNA of Jake Edwards's and Sandra Wells's are missing. All they needed was to find Jake and repeat the DNA test. It sounded easy by the way photos and the description of Jake Edwards that overloaded both TV and the newspapers.

I called Davis back and told him about Crandall's dismissal.

"By the way," Davis said, "I've been meaning to tell you something that happened in our lab. I thought you might be interested. You remember Sandra Wells, don't you?"

"Of course. How could I forget Sandra Wells and her frozen embryo? That is our child. Jordan took her to birth."

"A few weeks after you caught the people that murdered Sandra Wells, the door to the specimen room in the morgue was open. Nothing like that has ever happened. Nothing was disturbed, so I didn't think much of it," Davis said.

"Did they take anything?" I asked.

"I don't know what they were after."

"Knowing the DNA of the infant is very important," I said. "There are sources available that reveal if there is something special with the baby's DNA or some medical condition that might require further treatment. That's why they get the swab from the cheek right after delivery."

"Aside from the cheek swabs, the refrigeration problem for the embryos was the only other problem at the hospital. There was minimal damage, but the city wanted me to look in order to see if there was anything that was missed. It turned out that they got there in time and the embryos were saved."

"Do you have a list of the embryos that were in the refrigeration?" I asked.

"Yeah, they're on my computer." After a few minutes, Davis said, "Here it is. Sandra Wells. There was no damage to the embryo."

"Any idea why someone would want to try to shut off that refrigerator?"

"None that I can think of. Pretty mean if you ask me. There is a fringe group out there taking stands against artificial insemination. I think it may have been the culprits."

I thanked Davis and hung up. Someone had been after my child, and I didn't know it. How could I be that naïve? I called Sennett.

"George, there is something about this embryo that was dangerous. Something someone wanted. Since it was never alive, it must be about something that embryo carried. We need to find out more about Sandra Wells and CRISPR. We need to speak with Earl Crandall and Jake Edwards. When we called Visionary Chemical, they said he was supposed to start work in a week or soon. They didn't know where he went. And no one knows where Jake Edwards is."

First thing in the morning, I was waiting at the front door for Sennett to pick me up. Jordan was tightly holding on to my arm. We had been through this before. Whether I liked it or not, somehow, someway my life was destined to be determined by the police. Before I left, I promised Jordan I would stay out of trouble. Regardless of what I said, I knew I couldn't leave any hint of finding our daughter left unturned. Jordan knew the danger of finding our child. "You know me too well, Jordan. I just don't know why this happens to me. There's nothing I did to start this. All I can do is finish it."

Sennett arrived, and I kissed Jordan goodbye.

"This is really tough, Ben," Sennett said once I was in the car. "I can just imagine how Jordan feels. But I know you would never sit by and watch someone else try to solve this crime. You would never be satisfied until you knew every detail."

I nodded my head. "You know me too well. I just don't know why this happens to me."

"There's nothing you did to start this. All you can do is finish it. Remember what I said. "We'll get Baby Blue back. Trust me."

"We need to find Jake Edwards first.

"Everything points to him," he said.

I looked at Sennett as he drove toward the expressway. "I guess. Where do we start?"

"If he is a friend of Reynolds's, we might find something from him."

"I guess. Where do we start?" I said.

"If Crandall was a friend of Reynolds's, we might have found something at his office in Grand Rapids."

"It's like there is something about this embryo that was dangerous," I said. "Something someone wanted. Since she was delivered alive, it must be about something that embryo carried. We need to find out more about Sandra Wells and CRISPR. It would appear there were only three people we needed to speak with—Earl Crandall, Tony Reynolds, and Jake Edwards. We don't know where Crandall is. When we called Visionary Chemical, they said he was on vacation and didn't know where he went. And Tony Reynolds is up in Northern Michigan."

I didn't know Crandall directly, but he was responsible for all DNA results on newborns at City. I spoke to a couple of people I knew at City, and as far as the hospital knew, there was never a problem with

Crandall. But no one had seen him for the past couple of days. This created a disorganization in the system and a perfect setup for disarranging laboratory studies.

Sennett and I called Templeton and told him our concerns about Earl Crandall. Templeton said he tried the office, but Crandall wasn't there and hadn't called in. It was another two hours until we heard from him. Something was wrong. He told us to meet him at Crandall's house. It was a bungalow on the north side of Detroit on a boulevard called Vassar Drive. Time had passed by this neighborhood long ago. It was hot out. By the time we reached the house and we walked to the front door, sweat was already running down my back. No one answered our knock on the door.

"What do we do now?" I asked.

Sennett said he had Templeton's permission to give a no-knock authority. That permission might have been the most time I've waited for anyone in my life. After an hour, Templeton and the squad car arrived with two officers. Templeton is a detail guy. Everything was by the book. After he arrived, he and his agents put on rubber gloves, pulled out masks, and then ordered me and Sennett to do the same. I could tell that Sennett was getting anxious with all the detail. Then they hustled to the front door with a metal pipe. After two taps, the door swung open. They walked cautiously into the living room. It was old, and there was a sour, musty odor in the air. After no one answered we called to anyone inside and then moved to a screened porch.

We went to the back hallway with the policemen in tow, and the smell was getting worse. Nonetheless, the sun made its way into the porch at the back of the house and shined down on two threadbare chairs and a battered sofa. The rest of the house looked like it had been ransacked, but whatever Earl Crandall decorated, organization and warmth was not part of it.

To be sure, we called his name again; there was no response. We finally found him stretched out on his bed in a back room. He was dressed in office clothes on his bed. There was no motion. There was also no pulse. A dead man. Looking at a nightstand, Templeton ordered all of us to keep our masks over our faces and study the room. It wasn't long before Sennett bent over, carefully picked up a notebook from the floor and put it in his evidence bag.

The smell in the room forced us down the hallway. When we stepped into the kitchen, we saw used dishes and food-stained pans in the sink. I could see Sennett had had enough as he pulled out his cell and moved outside toward his car. I followed him and waited as he called for a crew. When Templeton arrived, he bent over and picked up a gun on the floor with a handkerchief and put it in the plastic bag with the notebook. Then he clicked off his phone and put it back in his pocket.

"I've called for a crew and an ambulance," he told Templeton.

Sennett and I went looked at the shaky handwriting in the book with Templeton. It read: "The baby's DNA is the key. In a tube next to book. Too bad not everyone is here. I never had anything to do with those embryos. They loved guns, and I needed to repay for my education. It was sent with the DNA, Index SWD VC #20-9229."

I walked away from the others to catch my breath and wandered back into the house. In the kitchen, I noticed a plastic bottle on the linoleum floor under the kitchen table. It was for a baby. I went outside again. The dead body, the smell, and the fact that my child might have been there were making my legs feel weak. I couldn't think. Instead, I asked myself for the hundredth time, who would have done this. No one knew, not even the FBI.

In fact, there wasn't much for me to do. Murder was Sennett's department. I knew we needed to go to Visionary Chemical in Kalamazoo and Grand Rapids. After speaking to Templeton, Sennett waited with me for an hour, taking in the fresh air on the curb. Then I called Davis. He wasn't in, so I remarked ironically that they were going to take Crandall to the coroner's office. I didn't expect to hear back from him for a while.

Then Sennett and I headed to Grand Rapids.

Chapter 26

Michigan has three seasons—summer, winter, and road repair. That's why it took three hours to get to Kalamazoo. Sennett drove as I called Jordan. I told her we were on to something, and this related to Baby Blue's DNA. She was excited and just as confused as I was. Before I ended the call, I told her we were going to Visionary Chemical and that Sennett had bumped up the protection around the house.

While smaller than its neighbor, Grand Rapids, Kalamazoo has many attractions. It is more than just a small town near the expressway. It has the Kalamazoo Valley Museum that offers science, technology, and history exhibits, plus a planetarium. American and European art form the core collection of the Kalamazoo Institute of Arts. To the south, the Air Zoo Museum features vintage aircraft, flight simulators, and rides. For out-of-door exercise, the multi-use Kalamazoo River Valley Trail runs through the city, linking parks and nearby communities. It was all for passing time, but we weren't here for a pleasant visit.

I kept on asking myself, " What does my child have to do with someone we don't know and never had contact with?" When I had called Jordan to tell her what was happening, she had said she was going to talk to some reliable Feds she knows. For someone as proactive and protective as Jordan is of her family, her not being here with me must have been making her frantic. I couldn't stop her from worrying, but I was afraid for her. The people we were dealing with were potential killers.

I was getting more and more agitated as I worried about Jordan and Joey. The murder of Earl Crandall pointed to something far different from we had expected. If he had the DNA, it would have been in his lab. I wondered whether his notes were his or someone else's. We had to get to Visionary Chemical to find out.

Visionary Chemical was located in a modest two-story building off the expressway near the downtown. After parking the car, we entered the building. Oddly, there were guards at the front door. Sennett had called ahead, and when we entered, we were taken to Crandall's office by the company's general manager, Jim Prescott. He was wearing a red-checked flannel shirt with the sleeves rolled up, exposing two sinewy, muscular forearms and gave us a handshake that was like squeezing an over-inflated football. It occurred to me that the word lumberjack for him was more appropriate than director of a complicated, high-tech business.

My impression changed when we stepped into his office on the third floor and looked through a large window so a manager could watch his employees. It was almost like a football coach watching his players from the stands of a stadium. There was one thing I noticed as we walked into Prescott's office, the desk was clean—no paper, no pens, no clocks. It seemed a little strange for a manager.

I mentioned the kidnapping of my child but didn't get into the death of Earl Crandall. "This DNA processing is like ancient Sanskrit to me. I'm having a hard time with the results of the DNA tests," I said.

Prescott looked directly in my eyes. "I guess you could say that. I was shocked when I heard Earl died. It's very upsetting for everyone here, and from a laboratory view point, it's been difficult to get a hold on the DNA." He looked a little defensive when he said, "They didn't have courses on DNA when I was in school. It's hard for me to decipher, although it doesn't have to be. DNA is a *polymer* composed of two *polynucleotide* chains that coil around each other to form a *double helix*, carrying genetic instructions for the development, functioning, growth, and *reproduction* of all known *organisms* and many *viruses*."

"I might have a medical degree," I said, "but that doesn't sound easy to me."

"Did either of you know Earl Crandall personally?" Prescott asked.

We shook our heads.

"As far as I have heard, he was a smart and pleasant man," I replied.

Prescott reacted with a sad demeanor. "What a tragedy. He had worked here before. We kind of shared him with City Hospital. This morning we found out that he died."

"That's why we're here," I said. "There was an infant who was kidnapped. We're trying to find if Crandall was involved."

Prescott raised his eyebrows and placed his hands on his hips. "No way. Earl was a hardworking, God-fearing man. This is strange. Before he died, he called me from Detroit to tell me he sent back some DNA specimens to the city coroner. I asked him what it was. He said he was protecting a young infant girl."

"In what way?"

"I guess he knew someone who might put her in danger. He was afraid of something. I don't know what it was."

I asked, "If she was in danger, how was he going to protect her?"

"DNA testing can help."

"How?"

Prescott gave me the thumbnail sketch. "DNA was first used in forensic science in England to verify a suspect's confession that he was responsible for two murders. Tests proved that the suspect had not committed the crimes. It's like a fingerprint. It never goes away. Police use DNA nowadays as evidence. It can be picked up in skin, blood, saliva, urine, hair, teeth, bone, and other soft tissues. Even chewing gum."

We passed several doors as we walked through the building. All of them were closed, except for one that seemed to be giving off cold air.

"You're lucky to be working here on a hot day," I told Prescott.

His answer was easy. "It's coming from the DNA lab. We need a large room with near freezing temperatures. When it's hot, that cold air really feels good. Low temperature is useful in dealing with DNA. All the doors in the DNA building have a refrigerator room for a DNA test. It has to be cold, especially for our single-molecule TPM experiments. They are low temperature rooms because the flexibility of DNA strongly depends on temperature in the range of 23–52°C. It gives a more accurate result. Even though a specimen may be minimal, there could be enough for DNA typing. Furthermore, DNA does more than just identify the source of the sample; it can place a known individual at a crime scene, in a home, or in a room where the suspect claimed not to have been. The more victim service providers know about properly identifying, collecting, and preserving DNA evidence, the more powerful a tool it becomes."

Prescott said that in some cases, a DNA profile may have been created at the time of the crime, but it would have been much better if a match was found during the initial criminal investigation. "Newer techniques overcome former obstacles, thanks to current database technology, which allows DNA profiles to be stored and quickly searched. Alternatively, DNA profiling advances have also enabled law enforcement to exonerate people who were wrongfully convicted of crimes they didn't commit."

I looked at Prescott with his bulging muscles and eyes that were cold, hard, and flinty. I felt there was no help that would be given here, so I deepened the tone of my voice. "If Crandall knew something like this, why didn't he contact you?"

"There was a call. I guess he tried to, but it happened so suddenly. He was here and then he was gone."

Sennett took out a copy of the note from Crandall's house with VC#200-9229 VC4895. SWD on it and showed it to Prescott. "Tell me something. Do these numbers and letters mean anything?"

We were in Prescott's office and at his computer. He frowned at Sennett's paper and then went to work, checking at the computer and then thumbing through files in the cabinets in a corner. After spending two hours of his searching, Sennett and I were about to leave when Prescott said the police don't normally give out DNA information. All Prescott could say was that they knew that Crandall was the responsible hospital person on a kidnapped child.

"A guy named Templeton from the FBI called this morning," Prescott said, "and asked us to send the DNA findings we had that were associated with anything Earl Crandall was working on, including any DNA. I'm required to hand over the information on the infant who was kidnapped. The FBI uses the acronym CODIS, for Combined DNA Index System; it describes the FBI's program of support for criminal justice, the DNA databases, as well as the software used to run all potential criminal databases."

"Did you find anything?"

"We sent him all the information on Baby Dailey. One was noted SWD VC #20-9229-4895. I don't expect anything."

My hand started shaking when I heard the name Baby Dailey. "What about CRISPR?" I asked. "Could someone be trying to alter someone's DNA?"

Prescott seemed taken back by the comment. "We do CRISPR at Visionary Chemical for certain diseases. We don't just alter someone's DNA."

"Does that include congenital defects?"

"I've never heard of that before. Of course, anybody that is interested in CRISPR would read Doudna's Nobel Prize acceptance letter. We have tremendous support from the public. In fact, Tony Reynolds, the congressman for this area, is the guy you need to talk to. He has been a great asset in raising money to further our studies."

"How is it coming along?" I asked.

"We're making slow progress. It's hard to pick which malformation or disease would respond to CRISPR."

Just then, my cell rang. It was Templeton. He knew I was going to Visionary, but I didn't think his timing was going to be that good. I went to the corner of the room and looked out the window as he spoke. When I told him Reynolds missed out on a meeting with me, Templeton said he heard the congressman had a home in Northport, Michigan. He told me if I wanted to talk with him, go ahead; sometimes people talking with a doctor like me will open up. I told him I'd keep him apprised and hung up. I now had my marching orders.

After putting the phone away, I was about to leave when I saw a bunch of small promotional portfolios. The folios read "Tony Reynolds – Candidate for the US Senate for Michigan." I picked one up and gazed at the promotional handouts for the next election. "Mind if take one of these?" I asked Prescott. "We want to meet with the congressman. He has a home in Northport. Do you think you can arrange it?"

"Sure, I know Adrian in his office in Grand Rapids. She generally gets anyone in to see the congressman. And, yes, feel free to take a brochure."

I grazed through it and looked at his photo. Tony Reynolds looked the real deal in politics.

Prescott asked us to stay while went to his office to see if he could schedule a meeting with Reynolds at his house. After a few minutes, he came back with a smile on his face. "As I said, Adrian usually comes through. She said around one o'clock. He's not there right now, but he is supposed to be there later this afternoon. She said that if you want to see him, it'll be a four-hour drive to Northport."

"We've got the time. Thanks."

In an odd way, Prescott had lived up to his promise that he would get us an interview with Tony Reynolds. But a four-hour drive wasn't exactly a triumph.

We walked out of the office discouraged—all this going back and forth with nothing to show for it. Regardless, I picked up my cell and called Templeton. I told him we were on our way to Northrup to see Reynolds, and we would keep him in the loop.

He said, "I don't want you to break into his place. I'll notify the FBI office in Traverse City that you're on the way and that you are under my direction. We have to talk with Reynolds, but I think you could get more from him than we could. We're pretty sure he'll be there at one today. I know he doesn't want any notoriety. If got any, it'd be in all the papers, and we'd have a mess to clean up."

Before he hung up, he gave me the FBI office number and the person to speak with if necessary. Something told me this wasn't going to be pleasant.

CHAPTER 27

WHILE PRESCOTT PROMISED US A CHANCE to see Tony Reynolds, it sure wasn't a straight shot. Besides the long distance, traffic was heavy at that time of the day, and Highway 131 was filled back-to-back with people going to Traverse City.

After we left, I checked in with Jordan and told her Sennett and I were going to Reynolds's home. There was a moment of silence. It was getting hard to talk with her. Every time I called, I could sense the anxiety she was carrying was increasing. This time there was a moment of silence. I was determined as best I could to be positive.

"Where do you think Jake Edwards is?" she asked. "If we find him, will we find Baby Blue?"

"I don't know, but finding the use of CRISPR is important. We're onto something. It must have something to do with the kidnapping. I know it's hard, but we have to think positively."

In spite of the possibilities with CRISPR, I tried to keep myself under control. The thought of the possibility of someone doing this to my child made me even more angry and more frustrated than I had ever been in my life.

Jordan brought me back to reality. "How does this guy Reynolds fit into helping Nobel Prize winning research?" she asked.

"Funny you should ask. In searching out Reynolds, I got to look at his record in the House of Representatives. As I mentioned, he's an archconservative and a poster advocate for gun usage. He also is involved with helping develop research in a company called Visionary Chemicals, and they are involved with DNA. These are the elements that Earl Crandall was involved with."

"Why is that important?"

"Jordan, Reynolds is all over the place in Grand Rapids. How do you figure a man who has never supported women's rights and supports owning guns is also philanthropic in supporting education, food banks, and healthcare? In fact, he donated a whole wing to a major hospital in Grand Rapids and has given grants for medical students, like Earl Crandall. Strange for a person like him. People in Western Michigan look at Reynolds like a god."

"Or maybe he is setting up a smoke screen," she added. "You have to be careful."

"I know. Earl Crandall's dead. Tony Reynolds helped him get through medical school and helped get him a job at Visionary Chemical. There may be a connection. It's hard to get an answer. I know you're worried. If it's any improvement, George will protect me."

"I trust George. Only I wish I could be with you," Jordan replied.

"Just stay in touch. You know how to find me. This time I'm driving to Northport with George to find Reynolds. Templeton told me it's an easy ride and if there was trouble, he has a backup in Traverse City." I knew Jordan was anxious and worried. I understood and promised to call her regularly. We needed to communicate.

Templeton was wrong. The drive to Northport took more than four hours. Most of the delay was due to a fault in the endless construction on the expressway. But once we got started north on US-131, we reached Traverse City in good time. Upscale stores, restaurants, and a few high-rise buildings all gave the impression of a growing, vibrant city.

Sennett drove, and I kept looking out the car window and wondered why would someone kidnap my daughter? Why does this have something to do with Jake Edwards? What was the purpose and how does CRISPR relate to all of this?

My first inclination was to call Jordan. I needed to tell her. After she picked up the second ring, I told her we were okay and in Northport.

She sounded sleepy. "Where do you think Jake Edwards is?" she asked. "Do you believe that if we find him, we will find Baby Blue?"

"Maybe finding the use of CRISPR is the real test."

"Why do you say that?" Jordan asked.

"Jake's record is clean, regardless of his political leaning."

"What do we do?"

"You'll have a tough time finding anything illegally based on the information you have. Not liking his politics is a weak excuse for incarceration."

"We need to find out everything we can on Reynolds," she said. "Can you do it?"

"I'm going to talk with Templeton. You know the FBI is going to investigate everything," I said.

"I have one other thing to say."

"What?" I asked.

"Based on what I saw, I believe our child is alive."

"How do you know?"

She responded quickly. "I don't know for sure, but somehow, someone is leaving us a message. CRISPR is used on live people. If our child has been kidnapped, then someone wants to do something with her DNA. But why?"

"That is the question," I said. "If Jake Edwards is involved, what is he trying to do? Someone must want her DNA. We'll know nothing until we interrogate him. I know one thing; Tony Reynolds and Jake Edwards know each other."

"I'm relieved that at least you found something," Jordan said. "So you think she is alive?"

"I don't want to give you false hope, but it's possible." I was taking deep breaths. I decided to change the subject. "By the way, how are you and Alicia getting along?"

"Great. She is such a nice person. George is lucky." As she spoke, I noticed her voice seemed stronger, and the feeling of hopelessness seemed to disappear. Since Sennett was sitting next to me, he was in on only one end of the conversation, I said, "Cool your jets, Jordan. George is a slow mover." I could hear Jordan laughing. Then she told me to be careful.

When I clicked off, Sennett looked at me as if I didn't know him. "What's this about me being a slow mover?" he asked.

"Oh, nothing. I was referring to your skills with women."

"Yeah, sure," he retorted with a tinge of cynicism. Then he asked, "Why would someone kidnap the baby? Was there something wrong with her, like her DNA?"

"I've asked myself the same question a million times. Your guess is as good as mine," I answered. "I wouldn't know what the consequences would be. The baby appeared totally normal. I've read about CRISPR and the Cas9 enzyme. They are used to change genetic make-up. If it was done, I have no way of knowing whoever did this, and while I could fantasize something off the wall, I have no understanding of what it means. There is no abnormal DNA of my daughter that I know of."

"What about the phone number?" Sennett said.

"Why would Carlyle have Crandall's name in his office file?" I asked.

"I tried to get hold of him, but there was no answer. Then I checked with City Hospital. I didn't find much."

"There's one other thing," I said. "When I looked at the screenshot, the card had three circles on it, red, white, and blue. I don't know what it means."

Sennett pulled out the paper and looked at it. "There are three circles floating on a cloud, but no colors. It's like the symbol of Visionary Chemical."

I looked at the paper closely. "I've seen this before, but I don't remember where."

The brain works in different ways for different people, but the ability to remember is constantly in motion. Sometimes you forget what you had seen in an object, and twenty minutes later you remember it. In my case, I had Knudsen. I called him and by talking and looking for an answer, he suddenly remarked that he had checked out Visionary Chemical.

"I called the US Trademark registration, and they confirmed that the three circles over the sun belongs to Visionary Chemical. They're near Kalamazoo, Michigan."

"We know about the company," I said. "They provide hospitals with chemical data, like confirming concentration of saline in intravenous medication and monitoring heart issues in the hospital."

"That sounds kind of mundane to me. Is that all?"

"Visionary also provides kits for all kinds of things in a hospital, you know, monitoring for in-patient diabetics, making sure patients on anti-coagulants are maintaining acceptable coagulation, and proper feeding either from a feeding tube or oral intake. They also develop systems for data recovery of patients with rare diseases."

Suddenly I remembered. "That's it," I shouted. I saw it in Margaret Edwards's house. I don't know what the relevance is, but I think his mother worked for the company."

"What hospitals do they have as clients? Is City Hospital one of them?"

There was a pause on the line as he looked. After a few minutes he came back on the phone. "That's one of them. The medical director is Jim Franklin. He wants to speak with you. I gave him your cell number. He's going to call you."

I know Jim Franklin. He was the chief medical doctor at St. Vincent. Now he runs City Hospital. I called him, and we discussed what happened. It didn't take long before he sent my cellphone a list that described the tests she had. There were DNA findings. Apparently, they found neither the DNA reports of the parents, Jake Edwards and Sandra Wells. Also missing was the DNA from the delivery of my kidnapped baby.

It didn't take long to reach him.

"How could this happen, Jim? Who has access to this information?"

"First of all my heart goes out to you and Jordan over this. I'll help you in any way I can."

"What about the DNA?"

"The DNA from your child was never directly submitted to us. It must have been taken during the kidnapping. We have rigorous rules to protect this happening.

"Who is responsible?" I put my phone on speaker and my body responded with a throbbing sensation in my head.

"One place where this could have happened was with a person who was impersonating an employee."

"If we believe he is the man, as far as we know that individual is dead. Shot to death outside of Cadillac, Michigan. They found him dead on a desolate road. Think of the people who have been around your baby who died. Sandra Wells is dead. Now we find Earl Crandall, the guy that was supposed to make sure the DNA was sent to the lab, is dead. I suppose some DNA could be retained from Jake Edwards, if he is still alive. All we need to know is where to find him. If we find him, I'm sure someone is going to check this CODIS index."

"To be sure, we covered all the possibilities, I've checked out Visionary Chemical," Franklin added. "This is a specialty medicine company that develops new ideas in treating cancer using DNA. From what I've read, they're legit. Now with all that has happened, I'm not so sure, and I'm sure you're feeling the same way."

"What the hell does that mean?" Sennett asked. "Every lab in the country wants to do that. How did Earl Crandall get the job?"

"Apparently working for City Hospital is dangerous. This guy, Crandall, was helped by Tony Reynolds to get a job working at City. They talked about funding research at Visionary Chemical. That is Reynolds's project. It's given him a lot of notoriety."

"As far as I understand, they have developed some new ideas on immuno-therapy. I'm not a doc, so it's over my head, but they must be going in the right direction. They even received grants from the government. I checked it out. It's a company that is funded in large part by Tony Reynolds. He's the guy who paid for Crandall's medical education."

"Does that ring a bell?'

"For sure, being admitted to any medical school is expensive. It's a tight economy and grants are hard to come by."

"You're right. A fool and his money are soon parted. We'll have to wait until we find out who killed Crandall."

"He was kind of a recluse, like he never told anyone where he was going. One day he just disappeared. It was strange."

"Just to be sure, if Reynolds funded Crandall's medical education, are we going to meet him?"

"His assistant told me he would be there."

Chapter 28

WE SHOULD HAVE KNOWN BETTER. GETTING into see a congressman is not easy, in spite of Prescott making an appointment for us. Reynolds wasn't in Northport because of a "change in the schedule." We were furious, but I did not want a confrontation. Sweat gathered on my forehead and my hands trembled. What could it mean?

Shortly thereafter, Reynolds's chief of staff, Adrian, called me. I sensed that she was angry when I asked if Reynolds knew what was happening. She adamantly said he was never associated with anything to do with Baby Blue. It bothered me because she was so defensive and the abrupt way she hung up. There was a moment of silence, and then she must have sensed she had been impertinent and apologized for the mix-up. She said Congressman Reynolds was on his way to Northport and would be back in a few days. Probably figuring we would never use it, she even gave us the address.

We left the office, and by the time we left the building, Sennett had called Templeton. I listened to the conversation. Templeton said he had called the Traverse City FBI and told them we were in the area. That's when he decided we should go to Northport. Templeton figured it might be much easier to find out where Reynolds was without a badge. In the meantime, the FBI agents would be available, and he gave us their number.

When we got up, the weather on this sunny day was mild with a soft breeze from the south as we drove along Highway 31 on the west coast of

Michigan. Once past Traverse City, the road headed to Sutton's Bay on the iconic Michigan Highway 22. We reached Northport in the afternoon.

The breeze had grown with a few clouds over Northport, and the marina was filled with both sailboats and motor yachts. We turned on the street where Reynolds lived and made our way to a large, grey, two-story house overlooking Grand Traverse Bay. A charcoal-grey sedan was parked in the circular driveway.

We went up to the front door and rang the doorbell. A middle-aged woman with greying hair, pulled back in a bun, and in a red apron with the name Carol on it opened the door. We introduced ourselves as individuals looking for Congressman Reynolds. Sennett made sure to show his badge. When asked, she said her name was Carol Raines. Sennett introduced himself and then me. He told her we had been following a kidnapping, and Mr. Reynolds was a person authorities wished to speak with. He was careful to explain that a child was missing, and the congressman might have some information that would help the investigation. He was clear to state we had no interest in accusing Mr. Reynolds of any wrongdoing.

"I've worked for Mr. Reynolds for fifteen years. I know Mr. Reynolds. There has never been any such thing that he would be involved with. Besides, my husband is an FBI agent."

It was coincidental.

"We understand," Sennett said. "It's our job. We have no proof that he has been involved with anything wrong. But maybe he knows or knew someone that might help us."

As I said, my husband works for the FBI, and I won't do anything without checking with him. Come in while I call him."

We waited while she called. It turned out that he called Templeton. While we waited, I looked closer at photos displayed on tables in front of a large stone fireplace. They were similar to the ones I saw at Margaret Edwards home.

After fifteen minutes, Carol came back into the living room. "My husband said he wanted to speak with the FBI chief. He called Mr. Templeton, and he verified you two."

Regardless, we had missed Reynolds. Carol told us Reynolds had left for Muskegon yesterday. She said he wouldn't be gone for long. It wasn't that far away.

Muskegon is on the west coast of Michigan. It has a fine marina to hunker down in if the weather changes. But we didn't have to worry about the weather. There was a steady wind from the north, and the temperature was in the low seventies. We waited for a while talking with Carol. She took us around the house. The view was great from the Reynolds's large living room and looked out across Grand Traverse Bay and had a stone fireplace, high ceilings, and comfortable couches spread out against each other in the middle of the room. What really caught my eyes were the photographs of Jake Edwards and Tony Reynolds. I looked closer and noticed they both had the same turned-up ears.

After staying for a half-hour, we decided to go down to the public marina and see if there was any information from the harbormaster. We got there just in time to see him, a stocky man with curly black hair, wearing a Tigers baseball cap and a plaid flannel shirt, embroidered with the name Cliff Flanders. His eyes were hidden behind sunglasses, but his face was friendly. When Sennett went up to him, Flanders was taken aback. He acted like he had never seen a Black man before.

Sennett showed him his badge.

Flanders seemed to become even more nervous when I asked whether he had seen Tony Reynolds.

"You missed him by about four hours. He took his boat out this morning from its slip and left about a half-hour ago. He has a Hallberg-Rassy sailboat."

"That's a solid boat. There aren't many around," I said.

"Did he say where he was going?" Sennett asked.

"Muskegon."

"Why Muskegon?" I asked.

"Tony Reynolds is one of the best sailors in this part of the state. Like a lot of sailors, he likes to be alone. He likes it enough to win the single-handed Mackinaw Race. The man really knows how to sail. I saw him anchor his boat once to a buoy in a twenty-knot blow. As far as I can tell, he just loves sailing."

"Was he with anyone when he was leaving?"

"No, no one was with him. But, it was a little strange. He took a couple of cardboard boxes onto his dinghy. Good thing there wasn't much wind when he did it. But, like I said, he knows what he's doing."

I thought for a while and then called Templeton to tell him where

Reynolds had gone. He agreed there was not much to do but to follow him to Muskegon.

By car, it's not that far. By a sailboat, it depends on the wind. If Reynolds sailed overnight, he should get to Muskegon in ten hours. Templeton said he would contact the local agents to let them know what was going on.

We thanked him and went back to the car.

Chapter 29

The ride to Muskegon took three hours riding on US-31, and we arrived around noon. When we reached Lake Muskegon, we found every slip filled with boats, mostly power boats. There were a couple of sailboats anchored to buoys. After we checked in at the marina, I mentioned Hallberg-Rassy to the harbormaster, and he pointed at a big blue sailboat anchored offshore. We asked to go aboard. When Sennett took his badge out and showed it to him, he gave us a dinghy.

Once on the boat, we didn't see much—no boxes, no feeding bottles, no diapers. It was depressing. It seemed that as soon as we got close, Baby Blue slipped away.

Inside the boat, it was strange and eerie, and having found nothing, we decided to leave. Suddenly, in the darkness of the ship's cabin, a man appeared. I recognized him through his photos. It was Jake Edwards.

Sennett also recognized him from a photo and reached inside his jacket to pulled out his gun. He had a searing look in his eyes as he stared at the man. "Stop!" Sennett yelled. "If you move and try to leave, I will make sure you are going nowhere."

Edwards stood there with his hands raised at the side of his head. "I'm going nowhere," he said with a heavy sigh. "You can put your gun away. I've been waiting for both of you for over an hour."

I was so angry, I could have ripped out Jake's heart, but Sennett had his hand on my shoulder. I cracked my knuckles. It calmed me down.

Jake Edwards cleared his throat and then rubbed his hand on his pant leg.

"Why did you come here?" Sennett asked.

"I spoke to Cliff at the Northport marina and told him I was looking for Tony. When he told me about Muskegon, I figured you would be here when I arrived."

"Why look for us?" Sennett asked.

"I haven't done anything, and I wanted to tell somebody what I know. I owe it to Sandy Wells."

Raising his eyebrows and offering a questioning gaze, Sennett asked, "Why here to Muskegon?"

"Probably the same thought process you've gone through. Maybe the baby is here."

"How did you get in?" Sennett asked.

"I knew Earl Crandall. I'm a public defender, and he was a client. There was a case of someone harassing him in the gay community, and I had to go to court to defend him about a difficult situation in a fancy restaurant. When I did, I got to know him. That's when he told me about the kidnapping of your child. He said there was an issue about DNA that was missing. He said he was angry because he had been ordered to send the results to Visionary Chemical."

"What did he say about sending it?" Sennett asked.

"He said he was to go to Visionary Chemical and follow it up from there. He said it was against normal procedure, but he was going to stay with it." Jake's legs were planted wide and his face reddened.

"What did Crandall say when the child was kidnapped?" Sennett asked.

"He was very agitated, as if someone was following him. I talked to the head guy at Visionary. He said Crandall was fine, said this guy at Visionary was a jerk."

"Any idea of a name?"

"No, he was too agitated to ask."

Sennett wasted no time in calling Templeton to let him know he had Jake Edwards. He made it loud enough on the speaker phone for all to hear and went on to tell Templeton exactly what Edwards had just said.

"How did you find him?" Templeton asked.

"He found us. Jake Edwards came to Muskegon, saying that first he tried to talk to Tony Reynolds at Northport, but when he was told the congressman was going to Muskegon, he followed him just like us."

"What is the reason to see him?" Templeton asked.

"We have something in common," I said, "since he was the sperm donor and Jordan gave birth to the embryo. Jake Edwards wanted to help me in any way he could. He said I should see Prescott at Visionary Chemical. He didn't get a chance to see Prescott. But I did hear from Jim Franklin that some DNA was found in a CODIS data base from a case that involving Michael Edwards."

"He told me I should look Prescott up," said Jake.

"What did you do?" I asked Jake.

"When I called Reynolds's office the next day and said I was working with the FBI, his staff told me he wasn't there. I was frustrated at the thought of what I was going to tell your wife. Even though I read a lot, I was wrong. Instead, the next day, Adrian, Reynolds's chief of staff, gave me a tutorial. She told me Prescott was going to gift Visionary Chemical in order to develop CRISPR at Visionary Chemical. She said the future for this was unlimited. If investigators could inject an enzyme called Cas9, they could actually create new DNA by reducing existing segments. The reward for this is being able to correct diseases such as cancer by altering the DNA of the malignant cells. What I couldn't come to grips with is the possibility they were not using this for some disease. There was a possibility they could change whom a person is, or in this case, something about your daughter."

SENNETT AND I EACH GOT A room in a Hilton Hotel; Jake Edwards got his at the Holiday Inn and was under the watch of the FBI. I was confused and angry and hadn't slept well the night before. Listening to the possibilities was not a good combination for a restful sleep.

CHAPTER 30

The next morning, Sennett told me, "They found something in the folder on Jake Edwards. You'd better talk to Alice."

I called her, and she answered right away.

"I'm sorry to bother you, Dr. Dailey, but there is this piece of paper hidden in the records of Sandra Wells and the embryo. It was tucked in the back of a folder. I don't know what it means, but I thought you might know. It wasn't much, just a name, He Jiankui, and next to it, a phone number."

"Do me a favor, Alice. That's the second time about this article. Take a screenshot and send it to Sergeant Knudsen."

It didn't take long before Knudsen called me.

His voice was agitated. "I looked into the article. It's the same one on that Chinese citizen named He Jainkui who had trouble with the government by doing something on embryos."

"What was the something?"

"He was trying to gene edit the embryo to prevent getting HIV."

"How does that work?"

"It's out of my drive path. You'll have to tell me." Knudsen referred me again to the article with He Jiankui in *Nature* magazine and the use of *CRISPR*.

"We know there was a problem with the refrigeration machine," I said, "but we were assured there was no damage to our embryo."

"Why would someone kidnap her?" Sennett asked. "Was there something wrong with her DNA?'

"Your guess is as good as mine," I said. "I wouldn't know what the consequences would be. The baby appeared totally normal. I've read about CRISPR and the Cas9 enzyme. They are used to change genetic make-up. If it was done, I have no way of knowing who did this and no understanding of what it means. There is no DNA of my daughter."

"What about the phone number?" Sennett asked. "Why would Carlyle have a name like that in his office file?"

"I tried to get hold of him, but there was no answer."

CHAPTER 31

WHILE SENNETT WAS DRIVING, I CALLED Alan Davis again. It had bothered me about the article on He Jainkui and figured he might have some idea what that was about.

He answered sounding irritated when I mention the Chinese scientist. "You mean the article in *Nature* about the Chinese researcher who was trying to alter his child's DNA to prevent HIV infection? I have no idea how that would be involved with your child, but it is interesting on a clinical level. What do you know about the DNA?"

"That academic bullshit left me with nothing to say. All I had was my daughter, Jake Edwards, and a dead man we found in a house. One thing I have noticed."

"What's that?"

Having your daughter's DNA could be very dangerous."

After talking to Davis, I spent the rest of the afternoon talking with Knudsen. I asked him to see if there was a match on the DNA of Baby Blue to anyone beside Sandra Wells and Jake Edwards, the initial parents.

Knudsen called me back. "The lab found something unusual. They have a data bank called CODIS. It has all the DNA in accidents and unsolved deaths. In the accident that Michael Edwards, Jake's father, died in, there was a handkerchief that had DNA on it that was not found on Michael Edwards. Interestingly, there was some similarity to that found on the DNA of Jake Edwards."

"What does that mean?" I asked.

"According to the guy I spoke to, there is a possible relationship to Jake Edwards being at the site of the accident."

"But he had an alibi."

"The guy at the lab said all of the possible people involved should be checked."

"What do you mean 'all the possible people'?" I asked.

"Well, he said maybe there is someone who looks alike."

When he said that, I had one of those hidden ideas in your brain that you never take for real—both Jake Edwards and Tony Reynolds had a Darwin's tubercle. Was this just chance? Jake Edwards had a father. His name might be Tony Reynolds.

I put Knudsen on the speakerphone and told him Sennett was listening in. I was so irritated I accidentally bit the inside of my cheek.

"Lieutenant, I got the details on Michael Edwards's death you asked for. He was killed in a snowstorm driving on a rural road. According to the records, the car spun out of control in a snowstorm, hit a tree, and then the front end went into the Huron River. I'm sending you the police report. The front end of the car was totaled. A piece of glass from the windshield cut into his neck. There was blood everywhere. The coroner said in the autopsy there was evidence of coronary atherosclerosis. After the windshield shattered, he must have struggled to stay alive because there was a handkerchief next to the car that was soaked with blood."

"What did you find out about the DNA on the handkerchief?" Sennett asked.

"I had the lab check it against everyone involved with this case. It turned out it the DNA in the handkerchief was on Jake Edwards. Also, it matched with Tony Reynolds."

"How do you explain that?" Sennett asked.

"Since we don't know the particulars of what went on that night, we checked out all of the people involved. The coroner suggested the accident may have been caused by a cardiac arrythmia. They have all the evidence if we want to see it. There was an investigation, but no suspects."

Sennett thanked him, and I hung up.

"How do we know this involves Jake Edwards?" I asked. "Where do we go to find Reynolds?"

"There is a DNA that might be related to someone—Reynolds or Jake's deceased father. How we get the DNA could be difficult," Sennett said.

"There always is the option to check out the individuals who knew the deceased individual," I said. I called Templeton.

"As far as Jake Edwards is concerned," Templeton said, "he is innocent of anything related to the death of Earl Crandall and the kidnapping of your child. The only way to check the paternity is to get a DNA from Jake Edwards and his father."

"How will we get that?"

"We need to have Michael Edwards exhumed."

By this time my toes were curling. "How do we go about that?"

"The law states that any kin of the dead person who is over twenty-one is capable of allowing his father to be exhumed."

I was getting tired of Templeton. He talked like a university professor.

"An exhumation is when a deceased's remains are removed from their burial site and moved elsewhere, this can be carried out for both buried and cremated remains. Jake is the closest relative and is over twenty-one and capable of allowing his father to be exhumed. A deceased may be exhumed for a majority of reasons, through family choice, a police investigation, for DNA testing, to transport them to their home country, and more. To carry out an exhumation, you will need to apply for an exhumation license, where you will be able to detail the reasons for requiring the exhumation of a deceased. Besides that, you need to get an exhumation license application and have consent from the owner of the burial grounds, as well as all next of kin."

It's a lot of red tape, but when it comes to getting things like an exhumation, there are few organizations better than the FBI, especially when there is a kidnapping involved. The casket of Mike Edwards was opened, and a sample of his hair was taken for DNA analysis. Rather than taking it to Visionary Chemical, it was sent to the FBI lab where the other DNA samples from Earl Crandall were stored. It took a couple of hours, but by the time they finished, they had some answers. There were findings of DNA on a handkerchief at the site of Michael Edwards's death that were similar to those also found on Jake Edwards. But when he had been questioned where he was on the death of his father, he'd had a solid alibi—a friend had been with him studying for a bar examination.

Sennett and I went into a small waiting room near the laboratory and were joined by Jake. It's hard to stay calm when you're dealing with a crime like this. We waited a half-hour, and they then called us all in. The examiner, Bill Rogers, introduced himself as a physician. He looked young with none of the facial furrows of the worrying of a longtime doctor. In fact, he should have looked consternated from the DNA reports on the desk in front of him. But when he started talking, this was no novice. He said he had gone over the DNA reports of Sandra Wells, Jake Edwards, the exhumed DNA from Mike Edwards, and the DNA swabs from Baby Blue. "I checked the DNA reports," Rogers said, "and there was nothing to suggest that Jake Edwards had any of the same DNA of Mike Edwards. Ironically, Jake Edwards does have some resemblance to the DNA on the handkerchief."

There was a silence in the room.

"How could that be?" Jake exclaimed.

"DNA doesn't tell how it happened. It only tells the facts. You would have to talk with the mother. He paused a moment. Here was something else. The swabs from the kidnapped child as expected, coincided with those of Jake Edwards."

"What does that mean?" Jake asked.

"I don't want to be throwing out weird ideas at you," Rogers said, "but I have to tell the truth. It means the man you thought was your father was not."

Jake's face reddened, his eyes squinted, and anger consumed his body. "This DNA is bullshit," he said. "You're saying I'm some kind of orphan picked up in an alley."

"Honestly, I can only tell what I saw on the screen. To be sure we need to get the mother's DNA. At this point, I don't know who's the mother. We need to test her."

"I know my mother. She'll never do it."

Rogers remained silent. It was clear that he was uncomfortable with the conversation. He seemed reluctant to say anything else. Nevertheless, he turned to Jake and said, "I know this is stunning to you, but I have to tell you the facts. The DNA on the handkerchief at the site of your father's death had DNA similar to yours. It also had some of the same DNA as in Baby Blue."

I almost jumped out of my chair. "What the hell does that mean?"

Thankfully, Sennett grabbed on to my jacket and kept me in the chair.

"We're not suspecting anything, but it would have been complete to take Dr. Dailey's DNA to make sure he is not involved."

Of course, I had nothing to do with it, but if DNA is proof, I'd take it. Rogers tested my blood and Baby Blue's, and I had no DNA match. The question was whose was it? We needed to take another visit to Margaret Edwards.

Before we left, we called the office of Tony Reynolds and quickly found out he wouldn't be back from Northport for a few days. Jake said he needed to leave some papers in Reynolds's office, so Reynolds's office arranged for him to come over. Then the three of us headed back to Grand Rapids in Sennett's vehicle.

CHAPTER 32

ON THE WAY TO REYNOLDS'S OFFICE, I talked with Jake. "Let me ask you a question, Jake. Mike Edwards was your father. How did you get along?"

"I loved my dad. We did everything together, hunting, fishing, watching football games."

"What about your mother and Mike?"

"It was tough. It seemed as if they were always arguing."

"About what?"

"Sometimes I heard conversations that weren't so pleasant, but I couldn't always tell about what. I do remember in one of their arguments that Mom said something about my dad's gay friends. It was kind of ugly."

"What relationship did your mother have with Tony Reynolds?"

"They were friends. No big deal."

On the way, I called Templeton and told him where we going and we had Jake with us. As I gave Templeton the details of our meeting with Rogers, Jake nervously twisted the watch on his wrist. I told Templeton we needed a DNA specimen from Reynolds to see if it matched results from Jake. Templeton doubted Reynolds would ever sit for that—it would be a terrible story in the press.

When I finished the call, Jake seemed relieved, maybe even encouraged. After I told him Templeton's take on Reynolds likely not consenting to a DNA test, Jake agreed, mentioning Reynolds's habit of constantly promoting himself and was glad we had purchased a DNA kit for this visit.

We arrived at Reynolds's office, and Adrian greeted us. Jake said he had left in Reynolds's office a book he wanted to pick up, and Adrian let him go in as she returned to her desk. Sennett and I sat down in the outside waiting room. The door to the office was open, and we looked in. Edwards took out the swab from the DNA kit and rubbed it against the surface of a used water glass on the desk. When he was finished, he opened a small vial, put the swab inside, broke off the top, and screwed the top back on the vial. When he finished, he scoured Reynolds's office. In the corner of the room, Jake found an ashtray on a small table next to a leather chair. With a jackknife, he lifted a chewed piece of gum off the tray, put it in a plastic vial, screwed on the top, and put it in his pocket. He walked out of the office and thanked Adrian.

After leaving the building, we stopped for a few moments on the sidewalk in front of the building. Jake pulled out the two vials and gave them to Sennett, who handed them to one of the FBI agents waiting for us on the street. They said they should have the results from their lab in a couple of hours.

Sennett, Jake, and I stopped at a restaurant, had lunch, and waited for the FBI to call us. After an hour Sennett's cell rang. When he was finished, he looked up scowling. "Looks like we have a match."

When I asked what he meant, Sennett nodded his head. "The Tony Reynolds's DNA test partially matched your daughter's," he said quietly. "It also had a DNA match to both Jake and the handkerchief from the death of Mike Edwards."

I looked at Jake. He appeared stunned. It didn't take long before a tear edged its way to the corner of his eye. I couldn't imagine what was going through his mind. Was Tony Reynolds his father?

"I need to talk to my mother," he said quietly.

"I don't think that would be a good idea until we get more information. I want to know what his DNA was possibly doing on the handkerchief, which leads me to another question. Please don't be offended. Did you ever think Mike wasn't your birth father?"

Silence wrapped round us. I could see Jake was trying to get himself together. "I thought about it once. I told you they were always arguing, but I thought they were okay with each other."

"Did your mom and dad seem close? I mean traveling together, going out to diner, doing the things married couples do? Did you ever think she was different when Tony Reynold was around?"

"No, I wouldn't say they were close, not in a good way. But I don't really recall her acting differently around Tony. But, and this is just a little thing, Tony has the same little knob on his ear lobe that I have. I always wondered us having the same deformity on his ear."

"One time, a guy I knew told me he almost married my dad. Then he laughed and told me he was gay. It made me so mad; I followed him one night to see where he went. It was a gay bar in the city. I had a deep conversation with him about whether karate or judo is the best way to kick someone's ass."

"How did that make you feel?" I asked.

"I felt justified and then just filed it away, but it always seemed to me that somehow he was still part of my life."

"What did your mother say?"

"She told me that Mike Edwards was a handsome man and at one time she liked him enough to have a child. That was me. But if my mother liked him, I wanted to know why she liked a gay person. It seemed so incongruous."

"How did Tony Reynolds fit in?"

"As far as I know, he was always a friend of the family. He was, as they call it, a man's man. We did a lot of things together, hunting, fishing, and sailing."

"Did you ever think he was more than just a friend?"

Jake stopped for a moment as if he was studying "I was a kid. It only was later that damn ear thing made me wonder how we both had something in common. He seemed so happy. We did everything together, hunting, fishing, going to the ballpark and watching the Tigers. We always had good times."

"Who do you think your real father is?"

"I took a course in genetics and reproduction. There was a discussion about heredity and how humans are adaptable. It was not from one generation to another certain things pass from one to another. In this situation, everything fell into place, including my ear."

I stared at him as I spoke. "You know, Jake, in medicine, when you try to make a diagnosis, you always think common things happen commonly. If it isn't common, it becomes a red herring."

"What's that?"

"Well, red herrings aren't common."

"Okay, you still haven't taught me anything about the red herring."

"Sorry, it means when you are trying to figure out a problem, you might get into a situation where a red herring distracts attention from the main issue. How can we have your birth and not know your father? There is a similarity between your DNA and that of Tony Reynolds's. Then we have a child kidnapped, and she has DNA that might be associated with Tony Reynolds. Lieutenant Sennett, here, is going to work on this. We're going to need your help. We found nothing in Mike Edwards's DNA that would have been given to your embryo. But there was DNA from you when you agreed to be a donor. That same DNA was found in the swab after the baby was delivered. That was in your sperm that was passed to my daughter. In addition, there was some parts of your DNA in the handkerchief where Mike Edwards died. That DNA seems to be associated with Tony Reynolds. Your mother is the only one whose DNA we haven't seen."

"Do you have any ideas?"

"Lieutenant Sennett is with us. We're both going to try to get that red herring."

Jake put his head in his hands. There could be no consolation, only a painful reality.

"Were you close to Tony?"

Jake seemed to slump on his chair. "We had some good times. He pushed me to go to law school. He said I'd make a great lawyer."

"Are you?"

"Well, when your father is gay, you have to take a different look at life. Tony was great to be around, but he was always deriding gays. I tried to make him look in a different direction, but it didn't work. Eventually, I let it alone. But when I was in law school, there was always some asshole who would make a dirty remark. I would never let it go, and I got into a lot of fights. I almost got kicked out of school because of it. Eventually, I worked it out and tried to live a normal life."

"What about your mother? Do you think she knew Mike was gay?"

"Now that I look back, she must have known. I never asked. I was a kid. If you want to get something like her hair, that could give us her

DNA. I have to find out. I'm a lawyer. I believe in the truth. People have died. I don't think I can live with myself if I don't find out. Where do we start?"

"I'm guessing we need to go back to see my mother."

Chapter 33

Sennett and I took off to see Margaret Edwards again, this time with Jake. And Templeton would be coming with a couple of agents.

Not much had changed since our last visit. It took two hours to get to Margaret's home. As we got out of the car, the door opened, and Margaret Edwards came out to the front steps, along with Templeton. As Jake got out, I could see the smile on her face. Jake seemed to be happy he was here.

Margaret stepped forward and faced Jake. She reached out to put her arms around him, but he backed away. "You look so grown up. I could hardly recognize you."

"A person gets that way when he is being chased for something he didn't do," Jake said.

Anticipating an argument, Templeton stepped forward and showed his badge. "We checked where you were on the day of the kidnapping. You were in court on that day and at that time. The FBI is not interested in incarcerating you for something you didn't do."

Margaret invited all of us into her house. I looked at the photos and paintings on the walls. They hadn't changed. Then I looked at Jake, and his body seemed to relax.

"The reason we came today," Templeton said, "is to discuss results of some DNA tests." He described the testing that Earl Crandall and the FBI had performed. "The results may implicate your son. He had

DNA testing as a sperm donor for the child that was kidnapped. That DNA was found in a national data base called CODIS. We ran a DNA on an object that carried Congressman Reynolds's DNA. He's the congressman from Grand Rapids. Your son, Jake, has DNA that matches Reynolds's DNA. "Your deceased husband, Michael, had no evidence of a Reynolds's DNA. There was also a Reynolds's DNA in a handkerchief found at the scene of Michael Edwards's death. In criminal cases, having a DNA can lead to solving crimes, but don't get me wrong. This CODIS was found on a handkerchief at the site of the death of your husband, Michael Edwards. The match showed no relation to that of your son."

"As I said, I had nothing to do with the death of my father," Jake exclaimed.

"We know. That's where the problem is. He explained that he exhumed Michael Edwards's body and took a specimen of his hair to see if he had any relation to the DNA at the accident."

I looked at Jake, and he seemed relieved.

"There's more to this," Templeton explained. "If the DNA was compatible, we might be taking a different approach. But there are questions as to whether Michael Edwards is your father."

"Wait a minute," Jake said. "I have only one father."

"I understand," Templeton exclaimed. "But your DNA is similar to that found on the handkerchief at the scene of the accident. We're calling it a Reynolds's DNA."

"I understand," Jake replied. "I never did and never would ever harm my father. I loved and worshiped him."

"I can understand," Templeton replied. "The DNA from the baby was similar, and it was also on the handkerchief at the site of Michael Edwards's death. We don't know how it got there, unless there was another person with the Reynolds's DNA."

"What are you getting at?" Jake asked.

Templeton replied, "Jake, when you were born, DNA testing was not done routinely. There are, however, signs of possible relationship with your friend, Tony Reynolds. As I understand it, Dr. Dailey here has told me that the malformation of your ear is called Darwin's tubercle, and it is hereditary."

"Wait a minute," Jake exclaimed. "Are you telling me that Tony Reynolds is my father?"

"All I'm saying at this point is yours and Tony Reynolds's DNAs are similar."

Jake looked over at his mother. "Is that true, Mom? I loved Dad, and you were always aloof. When I was growing up, Tony Reynolds was at our house regularly. Tony and Dad were friends. Tell me the truth, Mom."

"This has to be a mistake," Margaret said. "We're talking about a birth twenty some years ago. How did they get a DNA on Tony?"

"I found it on some chewing gum he left in an ashtray at his office."

Margaret Edwards was quiet and didn't seem as aloof she was when we arrived. It was as if she was hiding something. In fact, it seemed that her eyes darted from one wall to another, looking for a place to hide. I told her about the DNA found at the scene of her husband's death. Her eyes continued to move constantly, as if she tried her best not to let her emotions take over. Either it was a habit, or something was bothering her. I asked her if there was something she wanted to tell us.

She shook her head and said, "I don't know anything about DNA. All I know is there is something to do with a missing child."

I thought about what Alan Davis had said. Regardless of what you think, you can't fight the facts. There was a CODIS alert, which means a DNA structure from a crime scene matches a DNA profile in the data blank.

There was something else. I couldn't stay away from Jordan any longer. I made the four-hour drive, and Sennett spent his time watching Jake Edwards. When I came into the house, Jordan was excited. She clung to me with tears falling from her eyes. It lasted for a few minutes, but when I mentioned Jake Edwards and the DNA findings to her, she said that the investigation had made her feel she was doing something positive.

"I looked into all of this guy Reynolds's business affairs, including his charitable contributions. It's interesting that he has given ten million dollars to the Voight Foundation."

"What's that?

"It's a think tank that does biochemical research. A large part of their programs has to do with new drugs for chemotherapy."

"Okay. Let's call them and see what they have."

"We will. But I saw something else while looking over my emails. It was a statement from a renowned cancer center on the East Coast, praising the work it has done treating cancer in conjunction with immunotherapy."

She took me to her computer and pulled up a screen, entitled CRISPR, on the internet. "From what I've read about CRISPR, I suspect it has something to do with combined therapy with DNA. We have to start digging. The first place is the medical center."

We were both exhausted. But not Joey. I could tell he missed me. We went out in the backyard and threw the football. By the time we finished, he still wanted to play. But I convinced him to call it a day since he had school tomorrow. There was no argument there. Once in bed, he was asleep in a few minutes.

Sleep was all I needed. After a peanut butter sandwich and a shower, I collapsed with Jordan in the bedroom. I awakened the next day with my arms around her warm body. We made love, and not that I'm naïve, I realized how much I had missed her in the past four weeks. Regardless, the comfort I had holding on to her body was worth my search for our baby.

Chapter 34

It was getting late when Jake, Sennett, and I went to Prescott's office. He was behind his desk and partially hidden by a stack of folders. When he got up, wearing a tight wife beater, he seemed even more intimidating than when we first met.

I asked him if we could see the files on Earl Crandall. He complied, and Sennett and I went through them. After an hour looking at paperwork, we found nothing specific. Prescott got up and showed us the way to the elevator toward the refrigerated laboratory. We had seen it all before. But as we turned a corner, I saw a white plastic something on the floor. When I looked closer, it appeared to be a pacifier. My pulse rate jumped. I yelled at Prescott. "Where is she? Where is my daughter, you prick?"

"Walk down this hall," Prescott said. "I'll be behind you. I think you will be happy. Both of you, put your hands behind your heads. If either of you makes a move, you're not going to see tomorrow. And I'm not a prick. I am the future."

Sennett put his gun back in his holder, and I walked behind him. We came to the DNA room. As we stayed in the empty hall, I felt the cold air. I turned to Sennett, and suddenly, a man appeared from around the corner. His face was familiar, but I couldn't place it. He wore a navy-blue jacket with a red, white, and blue pin on the lapel, grey trousers ,and a face that displayed the arrogance of someone used to getting what he wanted. Then I placed it. "You're Tony Reynolds, right?

"That's none of your business."

Jake's nostrils were flaring as he planted his legs wide in front of him. " It is because of you that I'm here."

Reynolds jerked his head up and stared at Prescott.

Jake wasn't done with Reynolds. "You're my father, aren't you."

Reynolds stood stiff. "Wait a minute. That's a pretty bold statement from a lawyer. You're just throwing something on the wall to see if it sticks. How did you get here? Did you ask Margaret?"

"Not really. I've got your DNA."

"Since when did you become a doctor?"

"It all makes sense. You may have killed Mike Edwards."

Reynolds face turned red, and his eyes narrowed as anger consumed him. "You've got nothing. You're just a smartass kid, and you forget I am a very important man in Grand Rapids. What you say will go to the public, and you could end up in place you don't want to be."

"Is that a threat? The police exhumed Mike's body and found his DNA. No match to mine. But yours and mine do show a relationship. You fucked my mother, got her pregnant, and then played the goody two-shoes father after Mike died."

Reynolds shifted from one side to the other. The look on his face was flat, like he was facing a wall, not his son. "Look, sonny, you're going to pound sand for the rest of your life before you get anything. I am a hero to the public. By the time I get through with you, you're going to wish you'd never met me. I'll ruin your life, your career. Maybe you'd better talk with your mommy before you start playing a hot shot."

I couldn't stand Reynolds's arrogance.

Jake did not appear to be nervous. "Leave her out of this. You killed Mike Edwards. Now you've got to pay. You want no one to know I have your DNA. You must have hated gays, and that's why you had that embryo incubator damaged. Without with my DNA, no one could connect you to me—except for the baby from my sperm. We found that the kidnapped baby has your DNA, because it's part mine. I get it now why you want CRISPR. There was a handkerchief at the spot where Mike Edwards died. According to the tests, it had your DNA on it. That's why you had Crandall try to wreck the embryo incubator. That didn't work. When Crandall heard we were checking the DNA on the newborn, he wanted to change the child's DNA. Crandall knew too much after Baby Blue was kidnapped."

Reynolds would have none of this. "I think you and your friends are on a short trip to see their maker. Mr. Prescott, show these gentlemen to their last room."

Chapter 35

Prescott stood in front of Jake, Sennett, and me. Before any of us could respond, Prescott pushed us into the dark, empty room. The door slammed behind us. In the pitch dark, I tried to open it, but the door was now locked. I was shivering and both of us had only one weapon, our cell phones, but they were useless—no service in this room. We were trapped.

Sennett put on his phone's flashlight, and suddenly, we all saw what a murderous situation we were in.

"George, we need to save our cell phones for light." Glancing around the room, I saw nothing that would aid us.

"We'll take turns. On the wall, I noticed a hammer, screwdriver, and pliers."

"How do you expect to open the door?"

"We won't. Someone has to do it for us."

"I've been here before," Jake said. "Those doors are heavy. Our best chance is to use the screwdriver on the hinges and take out the pins." Jake took the screwdriver and a hammer off the wall and pulled out both pins. The door didn't move.

"We've got to stay together and fend off the temperature," Jake said. "I remember there's a Bunsen burner here." He shined his flashlight on the workbench and found it. "All we need is a match. There's got to be one if there's a burner."

Sennett reached into his pocket and pulled out a lighter. It didn't take long for the burner to ignite. Soon the light and heat from the burner helped improve our condition. However, the lack of phone lines brought us back to reality.

"How can we get out of this hellhole?" Sennett said, shivering in the dark.

"We're going to get out," I said. "We'll find a way. My child is here. We're going to get out. I know it."

"Let me try," Sennett said. They taught us at the academy on the ways to open a locked door. It's getting cold in here. We'd better hurry up. I don't know if this is going to work." He pulled out a bobby pin, bent it to a ninety-degree angle, and shaved off the rubber tip on the straight end with a knife. He inserted that end into the keyhole. "Now, I bend the pin so it's flush against the outside of the lock and then make a hook at the end of a second pin to create a tension lever. I need to hold the tension lever in place at the bottom of the keyhole to prevent the pins in the lock from falling back into place while I lift them with the first pin. Then I'll turn the lever counterclockwise to open the door."

"Unless I've missed your gender, do you always carry a bobby pin?" I asked.

"Funny you should ask. It's part of my kit. I've always carried it when I'm working."

I shined my cellphone on the lock as he worked. He turned the lever counterclockwise, and suddenly the door opened. We walked toward Prescott's office.

There was no end to the frustration and anger I had. My child was here, but where? I turned to Sennett. "What will we do?"

"We're going to stand next to his office and wait for him to come out. If he's there, it'll be our only chance to get him. Time is against us."

Jake took one side of the door, and Sennett the other. There was no noise. I used my foot and banged it against the door. It sprang open. Inside were Prescott and Reynold. Prescott looked frantic as he jumped from his chair and ran toward us. He had a gun in his hand and pointed it at me. I looked again, there was a third person, Margaret Edwards.

"I don't know how you got out, but this is the end," she said.

Two minutes later, I looked up and saw Jordan. I was stunned. "How did you get here?"

"Remember that device on my cellphone that tells me where you are? You've been here without communicating."

"Forget the bullshit," Margaret said. "Your man was too good. We need to get rid of him and his friends. They were too smart for themselves. Jake is my son."

Jake watched his mother circle around him. "You needed to kill people just to get what you want. Mike Edwards was a good person. He didn't deserve this."

"How do you know he was killed?" Reynolds asked.

"It's all in the DNA," I replied. "You must have missed the bloody handkerchief. Killing me won't destroy that evidence."

"You're a liar," Margaret replied, as she raised her revolver. "We've got to get rid of this guy and his wife." As she spoke, she raised her gun and aimed it at me. Suddenly, Jordan ran at Margaret from the side, knocking her down just as she pulled the gun's trigger. There was a loud noise from the gun, but I wasn't the victim.

Reynolds slumped to the floor. I stared at blood erupting from his chest.

Margaret threw the gun on the floor. "Oh, no, Tony! It was an accident," she screamed. Her face twisted in anger and fear as she bent over to reach the gun.

Before she could grab it, Jake kicked it away, and Jordan picked it up. As she did, I rushed to Reynolds's side and took off his jacket. Blood oozed from his arm, and his white shirt was red from top to bottom. I checked Reynolds's pulse. It was rapid but present. "This man needs to get to a hospital now!" I commanded.

With the help of Prescott, Reynolds stood up, and then Sennett took Reynolds into the elevator. Within five minutes, through an open window, the whine of an ambulance could be heard in the distance. I had looked at the wound, it was mostly soft tissue and did not look life threatening.

It also didn't take long to for Prescott to figure this was his time to make an exit. I tried to stop him. Instead, he started to run down the corridor. I ran after him, forgetting this was a giant, and I was a has-been jock. I caught up to him at the stairway and tackled him just as he was going to escape. He looked at me like this was something that had never happened to him. Infuriated, he tried to push me aside with a closed fist. The blow landed on my chest and stunned me for a moment. I staggered.

Panting, I yelled at him as he ran down the stairs toward a set of doors. "You're going nowhere, except to prison."

My anxiety, my fear, and the effects that had inflamed my family surged in my head.

There was another scream. It came from Jordan. "I think there's a baby here. I saw a pacifier and an empty bottle on the floor. Then I heard the cry of a baby."

I turned toward Margaret with an anger I had never felt before. This was my baby. "Instead of mourning the death of a killer," I stared at her for a moment and yelled, "tell us where the baby is."

"I don't know," she replied, only looking out the window at Reynolds leaving in the ambulance."

Rage consumed me. I charged at her. She was now an unarmed woman, and I could have killed her. I was saved when Templeton came from the back of the room.

"FBI," he shouted. "Hands up. Tell us where the baby is."

Jordan was my hero. I could hear the EMS car in the distance. Jordan came with me, and Templeton ordered his assistants to stay with Margaret. Templeton wasn't a big man and didn't equal the muscular body of Prescott. In most aspects I wasn't either. But I was focused on seeing my daughter.

We walked down the hallway into a small dark room with a crib. A nightlight was on in the corner. If I hadn't nudged the crib, the child inside wouldn't have wakened. One glance at me and she started crying. I turned the overhead light on, and in the light, there was the most beautiful child I had ever seen. The first thing I did was look at her eyes. They were deep blue. My eyes started to tear. Jordan picked up Baby Blue and held her in her arms. She was crying, but it was a good cry. I put my arms around Jordan, and the two females in my life rested against my chest.

Prescott escaped. Sennett returned too late with a pair of FBI agents. By this time, the whole building was filled with FBI and city police. I looked out the window and saw four squad cars at either end of the street.

"Not bad, Doc," Sennett said. "I think the public is not going to be forgiving. I'm sure as hell, justice was just served."

It took a few minutes, but after she recovered from the excitement, Jordan started to talk with me. I told her that it was her action with the gun that saved our child. She shrugged it off and handed the baby to me.

I could not avoid my tears. But I also had a feeling of relief I had never had before. Once again, she was ours.

I figured it was the federal attorney in Jordan that kept her quiet. That lasted for a while, and then she asked me a question. "What's going to happen to the kidnapper?"

I shook my head. "Reynolds's gunshot looked like a soft-tissue issue."

"This is going to be big news," Jordan said. "I don't know how they are going to play it."

"There is a handkerchief found at the site where Michael Edwards died. For a man like Reynolds, who is a possible presidential candidate, I suspect he wants no part of a scandal that is chasing him down. He might have killed Mike Edwards."

"What would you do if you were in that position?" Jordan asked.

"Get rid of the evidence. Change the DNA in one person who has his DNA, our child."

"How would he do that?"

"Read Doudna's nightmare," I said. "He'd use the CRISPR to change her DNA."

"We don't know if it has already been done. We need to check it out."

"That's where he has us. He may have been able to change it after she was kidnapped."

"And we're the ones who can find out now," Jordan said.

"We can't endanger our lives and that of the baby's. We need to set him up."

"What do you mean? Isn't that that kind of far out?"

"It could be. I had Alan Davis read the coroner's report. He said that Mike Edwards died from a coronary artery blockage. When he read the medical records, he found that Edwards had previous treatment from a cardiologist. One of the medications Edwards was taking was metoprolol. That's a medicine that lowers cholesterol. Interesting, Davis told me the coroner that did the autopsy found he had high a high level of metoprolol."

"Isn't that a good thing for heart problems?"

"It is, except if the patient is taking too much of it. It can cause intense muscle weakness. His medicine may cover up the symptoms of low blood sugar, including fast heartbeat, and increase the risk for serious or prolonged low blood sugar."

"Why would he take too much?"

"He wouldn't knowingly. Someone else might have given it to him in a drink or some food, and he wouldn't have known. These drugs are very small. According to the records, Edwards was in a restaurant the night he died. In order to find if Reynolds was buying the drug, we tried the same pharmacy and found in the records on the same day that a Tony Reynolds got a thirty-day supply that his physician had prescribed."

"That sounds strange, but even if he was in a restaurant, how would we know who gave it to him? It's been a while."

"You're right. We could call the restaurant he stopped at that night, explain there was a death, and see if they have any record of Reynolds and Edwards in their data base."

"Like what?" I asked.

"That's where you come in. The restaurant keeps credit card payments. We know the date it happened. We know the time and the city. That's a start.

"I spoke with Jake," Sennett said. "He said his mother and Reynolds often went together to the Campus on the Hill. He remembers because he wanted to go, and they seldom brought him along. On the day Mike Edwards died, Jake didn't recall being there, but he sure remembered the snowstorm."

Chapter 36

WHILE MY FAMILY WAS RESTORED, I couldn't buy what Prescott and Reynolds were selling. On site, Prescott said he had not kidnapped Baby Blue. Instead, he claimed that it was Earl Crandall.

The next two hours were frustrating. The restaurant, Campus on the Hill, had no desire to be connected to Edwards's death. That's where Jordan came in. The words "federal attorney" did not sit well with the owner, but Jordan had seen this reaction before. An hour later, the restaurant owner called and said there were forty people in the restaurant and bar that night. He had the records and would email them to Jordan.

An hour later the credit card information came through her cell phone. It wasn't easy, even for Jordan. "I'm glad he sent this, but you would think he would have wanted to cooperate more."

"I've seen this before," I said. "Places like that don't want that kind of publicity. Bad for business. I understand."

We sat at a desk and carefully went through the credit card names. After an hour, we were getting bleary eyed. Then Jordan said, "We've got a winner. The name is Anthony Reynolds. All we need to know is whether Reynolds had access to a sedative."

"How do you do that?"

"Most medical insurance plans keep a record on medications. What we need now is Reynolds's medical history."

I asked Jordan, "How do we do that?"

"US doctors across the political spectrum are protesting a provision in the Patriot Act that allows the government to seize patients' medical records without a probable cause or a warrant. The act prohibits doctors from telling anyone, including the patient, that their sensitive medical records have been seized. Doctors who violate the gagging order can be fined and prosecuted for obstruction of justice. If someone is running for public office, the person has to give his or her doctor's name and history. It is public information."

"How do you know that?"

"There was a congressman who had some peculiar problems in interactions with local politicos. I went after his medical records and found he was taking a medicine that could cause a problem on a dispute over local elections. It turned out that the medicine he was taking was making him disturbed. Being a federal attorney, I have access."

Jordan called her contact, and I listened. They pulled out Anthony Reynolds's medical records, copied it, and sent to her in an email. When she received them, Jordan printed them out. I looked at them, and everything appeared normal to me. The only medicine he was taking regularly was metoprolol for cholesterol."

"Nothing about his medical record is unusual," I said, "except for the elevated supply of cholesterol medication. In terms of drugs, the pharmacy sheet shows a minimal single dose, despite a large amount of the drug that was ordered."

"Could you prove the medication was the cause of the car accident?" Jordan asked.

"That would be hard, unless Reynolds panics. The only thing I can get is that he has not ordered any metoprolol, starting at a date after the death of Michael Edwards. The spin on the recent shooting was a disgruntled constituent. Reynolds is okay and does not want to pursue it any further. The kidnapping has been put in the unsettled bucket."

It was Prescott who really bothered me. He had left the scene, and who knew where he was now? I walked down the stairs and went outside. The EMS unit was preparing to leave, but I saw Prescott. He was standing nonchalantly in front of the park. The mobile TV channels had their investigators there.

As I watched Prescott, Reynolds arrived with his arm in a sling walking next to Sennett. I didn't wait for a discussion. Instead, I ran across the street to Sennett, Reynolds, and Prescott. I had no idea what was going to happen to Reynolds and Prescott. Before I could get to Reynolds, Prescott came after me. He positioned the TV people so only I was under scrutiny. I was blocked in between the EMS unit with Reynolds, this giant of a man, and a bunch of gawking people. Prescott reached out and grabbed me by my coat. I struggled to get away, but it was too late.

He had a pistol pointed at my ear. "You've got nowhere to go. You messed with Anthony Reynolds. Now you've got to pay the price." Then, he pushed me into the EMS unit like I was an animal at the zoo. My legs and arms were tied down in the back of the SUV. Next to me was Sennett. The SUV was started, and we'd be going to a no man's land of information that would ruin Reynolds's chances on getting the presidency.

Prescott nodded his head. "You're up against one of the strongest candidates for the US Senate. We oppose immigration, support guns, and want a balanced budget, and we will fight to get our people where they should be."

"Get me out of here."

Sennett pushed his way toward Prescott. "I am an officer in the Detroit police, working for the FBI. You mess with me or with the doctor here, and you're going to be in big trouble. Now untie him. The FBI is watching you."

The word FBI must have gotten the message to him. He untied me and walked away. It was cold outside, so I put on my gloves and crossed the street to where he was standing. He was doing all the talking to anyone who passed, including the press, as if nothing had happened. He was next to where Reynolds was sitting. From the way he looked, it appeared to be nothing but soft tissue that was damaged.

The TV guy got into Reynold's face and asked if there was any truth to his being involved in the kidnapping of a baby.

"Just the opposite," he replied. "This child was dropped off on the steps of the Visionary Chemical building. There were questions from the press as to how Baby Blue got here. The answer was that Mr. Prescott, who works for Visionary Chemical, claimed he found Baby Blue on the steps of the building.

Next, they questioned him on the injury in his arm.

"I got that trying to defend the child. Fortunately, I saved her life. Mr. Prescott called the EMS. I'm okay. The important thing is the child is okay."

"Is there any idea who injured you?"

"It was apparently an accidental shot by a woman I know

At that point, Templeton walked past Reynolds, who then shouted out at both Sennett and me. "It's just a scratch. You'll never get anything on me. I'm clean."

"Is that from you or the people who know?" I asked.

"I'm clean," he replied. "I would never even think of doing that. You don't know what you're talking about."

"The DNA findings say otherwise."

"You have nothing but air," Reynolds said.

"I have more than that. I have my daughter, and she will prove you are the killer of Michael Edwards."

"I'm getting bored listening to you. You're a barnyard doctor with little intelligence."

"Why did you kidnap my child?"

"I didn't kidnap her. She was delivered to me."

The fury in my body was taking over. My hands were shaking, and one of my gloves slipped out of my hand. As I bent down to pick it up, I bent my forearm, and with every inch of strength I had, I jolted my upper body upward and pummeled the bottom of his jaw with my forearm. I heard a strange screaming noise as he spit out blood and four teeth fell on the sidewalk.

TV cameras were on both sides of the street.

The EMS guy came over and asked what happened.

"I don't know. He must have tripped on something," I said.

"Looks like someone is going to need a dentist."

We got into Sennett's SUV and followed.

"Now's your chance to show me your two-block theory, George."

We followed and finally caught up to Reynolds. He got out of the car as I closed in on him.

"What are you following me for?

"How about kidnapping and assault on a city policeman?"

He came after me with a gun in his hand.

"Stop! Police!" I yelled.

Reynolds kept moving I ran after him, and Sennett cuffed him and called for backup.

I saw Reynolds take a gun inside his jacket. "Get low. He's got a gun!" I yelled. I dropped and rolled on the pavement behind the EMS unit, just in time to miss a bullet that ricocheted off the vehicle. From the ground, I saw Jordan clutching our baby and ease her way toward me. Fortunately, Reynolds didn't see her.

"You're finished, Reynolds," she said. We have the DNA from a swab taken at the baby's birth. It has your DNA on it."

"You're out of contact, lady. I defy you to check the baby's DNA."

"We already did and compared it to the swab Earl Crandall took after delivery. They match.."

"Who the hell are you.?"

"I'm the last person you want to see. I'm a lawyer with the Feds. And that's my baby you kidnapped. You may think you're smart, but not that smart. You killed Mike Edwards on that snowy day near the river. We have all the information we need to take you to prison. Give it up, Reynolds. You're no longer the chief. Your days are done."

The swag was gone. Reynolds must have known he had nothing left. His face was red and sweaty, and he continued to wipe his hands with a handkerchief. He looked toward the floor as the FBI swarmed to close in on him. Before they reached him, Reynolds pulled out his gun, pressed it against his head, and pulled the trigger.

After the shot, silence fell and then a woman screamed.

The son of God goes forth to war,
a kingly crown to gain;
his blood red banner streams afar;
who follows in his train?
Who best can drink his cup of woe,
triumphant over pain,
who patient bears his cross below,
he follows in his train.
– Reginald Heber

GENE RONTAL is a head and neck surgeon. Born in Detroit, he attended the University of Michigan, where he received his medical degree. After completing a residency at the University of Minnesota, he went into private practice in the Detroit area and began teaching at the University of Michigan Medical School. He is currently a professor in the Department of Otolaryngology/Head and Neck Surgery. His writing career started twenty years ago when he published his first novel, *Sterile Justice*. Since then he has four other books in print (*A Lethal Dose*, *The Cruelest Cut*, *The Police Surgeon* and *A Pre-Existing Condition*) and has participated in promoting them with book signings and radio and newspaper interviews. In addition to his mystery writing, Gene Rontal has published over fifty scientific articles, authored chapters in medical textbooks, and has been quoted in a number of lay publications, including *Time*, *Science*, *National Geographic*, and the *Wall Street Journal*. Doctor Rontal and his wife, Ellen, enjoy skiing, traveling, and spending time with their family.